THIS

PART ONE

Remy Dean

with

Zel Cariad

THIS, THAT & THE OTHER

BOOK ONE, PART ONE:

THAT REALM, WHEREIN WE HUME DO DWELL

To Seren
 Hope you enjoy
  & find the magic!
     Jeremy Lear 2019

Zel Cariad

Prologue: **Where to Begin?** ... 7

Chapter **One: The New Girl** ... 17

Chapter Two: **The Fair** ... 29

Chapter Three: **Dream-sharing** ... 47

Chapter Four: **A Stray in the Woods** ... 59

Chapter Five: **A Dog's Life** ... 75

Chapter Six: **The Name Game** ... 83

Chapter Seven: **Recuperation** ... 97

Chapter Eight: **A Visit to Grandma's** ... 113

Chapter Nine**: Just One of Nanna Ivy's Fairy Stories** ... 133

Chapter Ten: **A Frightful Night** ... 159

Chapter Eleven: **Wanted** ... 169

Chapter Twelve: **Deep in the Dark Woods** ... 179

Chapter Thirteen: **Meet Lee** ... 203

Chapter Fourteen: **Referencing the Stone** ... 221

Chapter Fifteen: **Going to Church** ... 239

Chapter Sixteen: **Preparations** ... 251

Where to Begin?

"I've read a lot of stories.

"I like stories about animals, and about going to other planets, and all sorts of stories, but I particularly like stories about fairies and elves and goblins… and unicorns and dragons and wizards… and knights in shining armour and fair maidens. I like to pretend that I'm a fair maiden, sometimes. I actually like it better to pretend I'm a brave and noble knight. A lady-knight. You get to go on more actual adventures then. See a bit more of the action. Well, I used to play a lot of pretend. When I was little.

"I'm guessing you did too. Read fairy stories and pretend… when you were little. Perhaps you still do the pretending, but you pretend that you actually want to do more grown-up games instead… but it is grown-up to read books, isn't it? And reading is a kind of pretending. Don't you agree? As we grow up, we pretend inside, by using our imagination…

"Well, what I'm trying to say… the point I'm getting to is… well, we all think we know about fairies and elves and goblins and unicorns and dragons and wizards and knights in shining armour and fair maidens… and even fair maidens in shining armour. We've all pretended to go to their lands, far, far away and long, long ago. It's like they're real in some ways. We've imagined grand castles and dark forests and friends and foes… it's like we've been there.

"So… I have a story to tell you… and it's all about the time I found out something…

something that's going to take a little while to tell you: about…

"About… words.

"Words like the ones you're reading, or hearing in your mind. Words that go right inside you, through your eyes and ears and into your imagination. Isn't it magical? I think you'll agree it's like magic when those words reach deep into your imagination and change into pictures, and places and… people.

"Well, this story is about…

"Oh, where to begin?

"I think I'll just tell you the story, my story, from the start. That way you'll get the whole picture. You can be there with me, in your mind, in your imagination… but that is part of what it's all about…

"It's about… Oh, I know how to begin a story! Especially a fairy story… and I have to warn you

– well, this is no ordinary kind of fairy story. You'll see what I mean pretty soon. This is a fairly scary fairy story. OK? So…

"Once upon a time, a long time ago in a land far, far away…

"Actually, the 'once' wasn't so long ago and the 'land' wasn't so far away. It all started a few years ago… and the story is still, sort of, going on. So really, the time is kind of now and the land is kind of, well… here. So…

"Once upon a time, in the here and now…

"There was this little girl – she wasn't so little. She'd been much littler in the past, she started out really tiny. As a baby… That's not so unusual. I'm guessing that you started tiny, too, and were a baby, once. Right? So that's something we all have in common – apart from liking stories – we all started out as tiny babies, right? Well, that's nearly always the case… So, the story is about the little girl who is, of course, me… but it could just as easily have been you.

"The girl in *this* story was called Henrietta Elinor Harvey. That was the name her mum and dad had chosen for her. Well, the 'Harvey' part was there already. That was their surname, and the girl thought that meant that her dad must have once been a knight, you know, Sir Harvey of… someplace grand. 'Elinor' was a name she shared with a favourite relative. A great, great grandmother. Henrietta had a grandmother, who she thought was great, so she wondered how great granny Elinor had to have been, to be 'great-great'… and 'Henrietta' was Henrietta's first name, all her own, she didn't share that with anyone she knew of. She didn't like to share all of it with anyone, at all, and preferred to be called 'Rietta'. Because it sounded a bit more unusual and modern, and it was shorter… and if she shortened it the other way, she'd have been called 'Henri', and that was a boy's name. Or a man's name to be exact – her dad was a Henry: 'Sir' Henry Harvey. She liked to pretend he was a noble knight of olde, although he was actually a 'part-time civil engineering consultant' – that's something to do with roads and drains.

"Right. I'll stop procrastinating. Could you tell I was procrastinating? It's a big word that means 'stalling', trying to put something off until later… just using the word, 'procrastinating', helps you to procrastinate! Because it's such a long word. You see, the reason why I have been… pro-crast-in-ating… so much, is that… well, I'm a little bit nervous about telling this story. And by the end you'll understand why.

"That's if we make it to the end. Because I have warned you, this is a fairly scary fairy story. The only way it could be scarier, would be if I wasn't here to tell the tale. Then you'd actually never know… and that would be just as scary, really.

"They say, 'What you don't know can't hurt you,' right? Well, of course that's not really true. They also say, 'Knowledge is power'. Well that's not always true either… because, somewhere between not knowing and knowing, there lies imagination. That's the key… the key that "unlocks secrets.

"It did, once upon a time, and it still does today…"

PART ONE

Come away, O human child!

To the waters and the wild

With a faery hand in hand,

For the world's more full of weeping

than you can understand.

– WILLIAM BUTLER YEATS,

The Stolen Child (1889)

Chapter One

The New Girl

Henrietta Elinor Harvey was looking out of her window. She felt happy because the sun was shining and there were pretty birds chirping in the trees around the little garden. The mountains, way across the valley, were dappled with the drifting shadows of small lazy clouds that looked as white and wispy as tufts of lambs' wool against the pale blue. On that bright, crisp morning, it did not even cross her mind that there were still places of darkness, that the brighter the light, the darker were the shadows it cast.

She did not know that before the next day dawned, she would have seen things that she never thought she would ever see, and that soon she would change forever. She would be changed from being a fairly normal little girl into being a very special and extraordinary person. It began a long time ago… but for Rietta, it all started when she met another very special and extraordinary person.

From her seat on the extra-wide windowsill, she could see her special place – the place where she liked to go and sit and think, and read and sketch, and generally daydream. It was a big, broad oak tree with complicated branches that swept low to the ground to shade several large boulders that were perfect for sitting on during sunny days. The ancient bark was all cracked and creviced with plenty of little nooks and crannies for hiding small, secret things, like special leaves, shiny stones and little rolled up pieces of notepaper with wishes written on them… and today would be a perfect day to visit her tree and perhaps make a meaningful pattern out of twigs and acorns on the big flat top of the moss covered rock… but as she looked out across the valley, across the silver ribbon of the playful mountain stream, she saw something colourful dancing in and out of the shadows under the branches and boughs of her special tree. She could not see much detail at that distance but she was sure there was another little girl in a purple dress, with something sparkling at its hem. It caught the sun-shiny dapples as she danced and skipped in the shade.

It could have been her. Same height, same sort of purple dress that she often wore. But it was someone else – someone not her, in her very own special place.

Rietta hopped unsteadily as she pulled on a pair of blue and pink stripy socks that overlapped her grey spotty leggings to the knees. They clashed nicely with her purple polka top. "I'm just going out to my magic tree, Mum." Rietta called, now downstairs and quickly Velcroing her shiny school shoes.

She heard her mother call, "Lunch in ten minutes!" as the door was closing.

Around the porch she rushed, down the side of the stone-built house, through the rusting iron garden gate and into the fields at the back. She knew where the little stream was narrow enough so that one step reached the rock in the middle and then it was one more short hop to the other side. If it had been really raining you could not do that and had to walk along the footpath to the bridge on the lane.

She ran on across the field and a few sheep ran away from her. As she got closer to the big oak, she could see the other girl was still there, the girl who could have been her, but was not.

Rietta stood for a moment and breathed, recovering from the sprint, watching the girl skip a little dance around the craggy trunk, toe-tapping in each little patch of sunshine in the leafy shade under the low, ancient branches. Rietta did that, too – step in every dapple of light as they moved, a dance with the breeze in the leaves.

The girl was fleet of foot, then the toes of her purple trainers pointed towards Rietta and stopped moving. The girl was looking straight at Rietta, head cocked to one side, her glossy brown hair partly swooshed across her dark eyes from the last little skip. Rietta was aware that she had not brushed her own fine blonde hair yet, and knew the light breeze would be lifting it away in all sorts of directions.

"Hello," said Rietta, a little bit too quietly, but the other girl must have heard because she said, "Hi, there," back. She also spoke quietly as if they did not want to startle each other. Her voice was gentle and her accent was from somewhere far way.

Rietta wanted to say something friendly, so she said, "I like your shoes…" and it was completely true – not only were they purple, they had lots of glittery details and they were lace-ups, with purple ribbons instead of standard shoelaces.

"Yours are so shiny," the girl said, stepping out of shade into sunshine.

"Oh, these? They're my school shoes… Do you go to school?"

"Not at the moment."

It was summer break. "Me neither!" Rietta said, then asked, "Do you live here?"

"Yes. I live here. In this tree – we have a nest on branch number seven…" she indicated by glancing upwards, her dark eyes squinting against the sunshine.

She was being funny-clever – Rietta actually liked that but pretended to believe her, "Really? Would you like me to collect some wool – to line it with – must get draughty in the nights."

The other girl smiled and held out her hand in a very grown-up kind of way, "We'd like that! I'm Carla."

They shook hands, "Well, pleased to meet you, Carla. I'm Rietta." It somehow felt like she was meeting an old friend that had emigrated a long time ago and just come back. Pointing back across the field, she said, "I live in that house, there… and this is my special tree."

"How is it special?"

"It's just where I come to play and think…"

"Yes. It is very… thoughtful here," agreed Carla.

Rietta was not sure how Carla would take such an idea, but she felt she could be completely open, "I think it's a magic tree," she confided, "A fairy tree."

"I think so too!" Carla did a little twirl, looking up into its leafy limbs, "Have you ever seen one?"

"I think I did once, when I was little. How about you, have you seen one?"

"No," Carla smiled, her cheeks dimpling, "I've seen hundreds! I see them all the time..." She skipped back into the shade. "I can call them you know."

Rietta followed, she liked the sound of this game, "Can you teach me how?"

She nodded, "First, find a handful of sticks and twigs."

They searched on the ground. She picked up stick after stick, discarding some and keeping others. Some were straight and smooth, some were forked or crooked. Rietta did the same and soon they both had a handful of twigs.

"Two nice curved ones…" muttered Carla and then took hers to the largest mossy boulder under the tree, where she carefully laid them out in a pattern. "There," she said, sounding satisfied, "Carla, Louise, Davies…"

Rietta had often used interesting sticks and stones to make patterns, so it only took a moment for her to understand what had been done: the twigs spelled out the initials: C L D.

"Now you," Carla prompted and Rietta did likewise. Carla watched and smiled saying, "H – E – H? I thought your name was Rita."

"Not 'Rita' – Rietta. Short for 'Henrietta' – Elinor Harvey." She tapped each letter as she said the names.

Carla moved the twigs closer together so that they all connected and it made a pattern that did, indeed, look magic. Then she reached out in a gesture that invited Rietta to take hold of her hands and said, "Close your eyes and say with me: 'On gossamer wings, As the mistle thrush sings, You live in my dreams, Now become real things'…"

In the shadow of the ancient oak, they held hands across the mossy boulder, Rietta closed her blue-green eyes, and they repeated the short lyric together. There was a short pause filled with the soft rustle of leaves overhead, the distant bleating of sheep, bird calls carried on the breeze. Then Carla said, "Now open them!"

For a second Rietta saw a silvery flitter of tiny wings, right at the edge of her vision. At least she thought she saw it, but when she looked straight at where it had been there was just grass glinting in a patch of sunshine.

"See something?" Whispered Carla.

Rietta nodded, "Thought so." She pointed, "Just there..."

A distant voice called, "Henrietta!" She looked towards her house and could just make out her mother standing in the open back doorway from where she had called.

"Dinner time," Rietta explained, "I forgot. Got to go. Will you come here again?"

"But you only saw one – there'll be more!"

"Oh…" she wanted to talk some more about fairies with her new friend, it was one of her favourite subjects. If only they did 'Fairy Studies' at school! Then she would surely be top of her class. "Call for me when you can – tomorrow. You know where I live."

"OK – seeya!"

Rietta ran back, over the little stream and at the rusting gate she turned to look back. Carla was still there skipping in and out of the light and shadow. Rietta ran up the garden path to the back door and pushed it open with a shoulder shove. She glanced back again and raised her hand to wave. Carla had gone.

Chapter Two

The Fair

That night Rietta was dreaming of fairies…

It was dark and yet the moon shed a pool of shimmering bright light around her special tree. In the dark amongst the branches were small points of light like Christmas tree fairy-lights, only she knew these were really fairy lights. So, she smiled up at them and said, softly, "Hello, is someone there?"

One of the lights moved downward from its perch and she raised her hand up to meet it. When it came closer, she could clearly see that it was a tiny, doll-sized girl. The silvery light was a halo that flickered behind and all around the little figure, like glowing wings fluttering ever so quickly that they became almost invisible. The hair shone silver and was as fine as gossamer, swirling on the eddies of air. Her clothes were woven from threads as fine as her hair and clung to the tiny form like wisps of smoke. Her little face… the face was incredibly beautiful, with the most delicate features.

When she alighted on Rietta's open palm, the fairy was feather-light and her mouth moved as if speaking, though all that could be heard was a sound like distant flutes. Then from somewhere within the notes of soft music, Rietta could make out words. The fairy seemed to be saying, "…live in my dreams… now become a real thing…"

Something changed, the tree and the other fairy lights faded and Rietta was suddenly aware that she was dreaming. She fought against waking as the tiny fairy lifted from her palm and made a beckoning gesture. Rietta was now aware of her bed sheets and, reluctantly, she opened her eyes. She was back in her bedroom at home… for a moment she felt severely disappointed. The dream had seemed so real and yet so magical and it had been so short. She almost wanted to cry. Then she realised something was different about her room. The shadows were all wrong, they were too clear and lit from the wrong direction. She turned her head towards the source of the light.

There, at the side of her bed, stood the very same fairy. Now she was much bigger, almost as tall as Rietta would be, though still so delicate and willow slender. Rietta did not feel at all afraid, the fairy was too beautiful and her smile was warm and friendly.

"Come with me now." The fairy's voice was still just as soft and musical as she spoke, "The spell won't last long." She offered a pale hand and when Rietta reached out to take it, she instantly felt weightless as if she was lifting from her bed. The air moved and the light from the fairy's wings obscured all else for a moment. There was a swirling sensation of flying.

Rietta's eyes adjusted to the brighter light. It was no longer night. There was cool grass beneath her bare feet and warm sunshine on her hair. She found herself standing in the middle of a large lawn, still dressed in her long, bird-print nightshirt. Brightly coloured butterflies flitted amongst the meadow flowers that grew through the grass all around. There were others there, some sat in small groups on the grass, others walking and talking in pairs. Most appeared young and many of them were also dressed in what looked like their night clothes. Something about the lighting made everything seem a little strange and unreal. The lawn was surrounded by small buildings, all slightly different in size and shape, though all made from pale stone with small windows and high thatched roofs. Not one had a corner or a straight wall. Some obviously had two floors, with upstairs windows that caught the light and these ones were like little towers, but most were low and wide. Piping birdsong drifted from dense green woodlands that rose up on hillsides behind the houses, and beyond that were distant, snow-capped mountains. The impossibly blue sky was dotted with drifting white clouds, their edges softly lit in silvers and golds. The sun was low and as she turned, feeling its warmth on her back, she saw the wide silver disc of the moon rising over the mountain peaks, opposite.

The beautiful fairy guide who stood before her spoke. "Welcome, Rietta, to my village," the fairy's voice was clearer and even sweeter now.

"You mean – you're an actual fairy and this is…" she was still taking in her surroundings, "I am, really, in a fairy village? Oh, wow."

"You are, for now. You are equally there and here – in That world and This world. This place is named Dreamers Dell. But you cannot stay for long…"

"What's your – ?"

"You already know my name!" the fairy urged, "Go on guess!"

"Mmm… oh, I don't know! Something beginning with… 'M'?"

The fairy nodded encouragingly.

Rietta continued, "Em… Mir... Me... Ma... Something like, Mar… erm, Maral?"

The fairy smiled a wide smile and nodded, "Yes, my name is Maral! And there is someone else here you just have to meet!" As Maral led the way across the flower scattered lawn, Rietta noticed that although she skipped so lightly on her feet, something had changed about her.

"What happened to your wings? Didn't you just have wings?"

"Wings?" Maral seemed to laugh out her words, "Oh, we don't need them in This world."

Because of the small windows, Rietta expected it to be dark inside the little cottage, but it was still very brightly lit. The interior was all natural tones, terracotta, unpainted wood, undyed linens and vibrant green vines that wound around posts and rafters, festooned with pink and lilac blossoms. The whole room smelt of their perfume mingled with the aroma of baking.

The only occupants of the rounded room were sitting at a simple, rustic style table, seemingly deep in conversation. One had her back to the door as Rietta and Maral entered, the other looked up and smiled in greeting. He was young and, although a boy, as beautiful and fine featured as Maral. His hair was just as long and silky shining, though absolutely black as the night sky and decorated here and there with metallic beads that glinted like the stars. His tunic appeared to be of some soft, leathery material with complex silvered patterns stitched into it.

"Rietta? Welcome to This world." His voice was quiet and clear. As he stood and gestured in welcome his other guest also stood and excitedly spun about to greet Rietta, who was astonished to find herself face to face with Carla, also dressed in her nightclothes. Pale purple pyjamas edged with white piping.

"Oh, my days!" Carla bubbled, grinning. Rietta could not think of anything to say, so they simply hugged each other.

"Please introduce me, Carla."

"Oh, yes…" she caught her breath, "This is Bren, my friend and…"

"Your friend," He confirmed and bowed deeply, his hair falling across his face like a curtain as he did.

"…and…" prompted the fairy at Rietta's side.

"Sorry, this is Maral. We just met."

Maral curtseyed and took hold of Carla's hand for a moment.

Carla smiled, "Oh, Rietta, I knew you'd be here this time! I just knew it…"

"You mean, you've been here before?"

Nodding excitedly, "I have so much to tell you!"

They all sat around the table and Bren said, softly, "You can talk all you want, when you are back in That world, where you come from. For now, I must apologise for our shortcomings in hospitality – we cannot offer you any food or drink, perhaps another time…"

"…yes…" Maral picked up the conversation, "The spell will end soon. You don't have long with us in this world, not this time. And we have something important to tell." Maral spoke as if she was reading poetry, with almost musical rhythm, "One day soon, both of you will find, your way back into this world. We need your help here. Only you are able, to help us in this. There is a danger that grows, ever larger and near. A threat to our people, that you can dispel."

"What could we possibly do that you can't?" asked Rietta suddenly serious.

"You are not of this world, and so you are safer here." Bren explained, "Unless it is stopped, what threatens this world will soon reach your own. We do not have enough time to explain everything, but you will know in your hearts, that you can and must help… us…"

Maral picked up the thread of conversation, "You will see signs, and we shall send a guide to you, into That world where you wake. The guide will show you the way, to get back to This world again – and when you come, then all will be explained, and you will know what you need to know, and you will be able to make your choices…"

"Won't one of you be our guide?" Carla asked.

"We cannot open the way," said Bren with a hint of sadness.

Maral smiled reassuringly, "You will know the guide when you meet them."

"Why us?" shrugged Rietta, "There must be plenty of bigger, braver people…"

"It was you who called to us, from That world…"

"The rhyme under the tree…" Carla whispered to Rietta.

"…and," continued Maral, "we heard you in this one. That alone shows us that you are special, and oh so well suited to this quest." As she spoke, Maral became slightly translucent for a moment. The flowers and the doorway behind could be faintly seen through her head and shoulders.

Rietta and Carla must have look surprised because Bren explained, "The spell is fading. You will find us again, but now you have to leave this world…"

Maral stood up and made a wide gesture with her pale arms, "Sorry," she said softly, yet firmly, "The spell ends."

* * *

Rietta's eyes were suddenly open, staring at her bedroom ceiling. She wanted to go right back to sleep and continue the dream, but she knew there was no chance of that, she was wide awake. She sat up in bed and swung her feet down to the cool floor. She could not wait to meet with Carla again and tell her about the amazing dream. But wait she must. With frustration, she realised that she had no way of contacting Carla in real life. No address. No phone numbers. No e-mails.

Rietta dashed to the window and pulled the curtain aside. The sun was only just up, the sky a bright, even paleness and morning mist clung to the hillsides and carpeted the valley. The top branches of her tree stood darkly majestic above the lake of milky fog. It was beautiful, but there was no real chance of seeing Carla in their special place just yet.

A heron flapped and glided, flapped and glided, like a dark prehistoric flying beast. She watched it fly low across the valley and disappear, fading down towards where the river ran. Other, unseen birds were beginning their dawn chorus.

"You're up early," said Rietta's mother when she came down and found her daughter already making a start with breakfast.

"I've made a big bowl of porridge," Rietta said, perhaps a little too enthusiastically, "...and the coffee's on – I heard you up and about." She thought that if she kept busy, the day might seem to go quicker and the sooner she could meet up with Carla again. She did say she would call again, or did she not?

Her mother was a tall, slender woman whose features were fine and balanced with wide blue-grey eyes that always made her look fresh and pretty, even when she was wearing her night-time giraffe onesie, and before she had brushed the frizz from her long, strawberry-blonde hair. "Well that's very nice of you…" she said, and asked, "Have I forgotten about something today?"

Rietta shrugged, "No, I don't know."

Her mother was checking the floral calendar at the top of a pin-board that was cluttered with postcards, notes and receipts, "No planned daytrips or visits?"

"I don't think so…"

The percolator started gurgling noisily and spluttered the last of its steaming coffee into the glass jug. Then the door chime rang out.

"Delivery?" her mother glanced at the kitchen clock, but Rietta had already dashed to open the front door and sure enough, there was Carla, her cheeks ruddy from the early morning chill and her rush to get there.

"Hi – It's not too early for me to call, is it?"

"No, no. Not at all. Come in and have some porridge with us. Would you like some coffee, or juice? We have cereals… and fruit…" Rietta plucked a banana from the fruit bowl as she passed and brandished it like a pistol at Carla.

Carla was still smiling when she said, "Good morning…" to Rietta's mother and sat down on the stool that was offered.

"Well, hello – ?"

"– Carla." Both girls said at once.

"Good morning. You're so bright and breezy! You can call me Sally," said Rietta's mother already pouring four glasses of grape juice, because at that moment Rietta's father bustled into the room still buttoning his shirt and looking flustered, "And this is Henry." She handed him a glass, saying, "Don't worry, you're not late. It's just we're all early, today."

"Morning!" he said and took a good gulp of juice. Henry had an 'outdoors' sort of face, etched with 'laughter-lines' at the corner of his sparkly brown eyes, dark close-cropped hair with a silvering of grey when the light caught it. He had not shaved, so his jaw was shadowed with stubble.

"Good morning, Daddy, this is my friend, Carla."

"New to the area, are you?" He raised his glass as if proposing a toast, "Well, Carla, stick with Henrietta, she knows her way around."

Rietta and Carla hurriedly ate porridge, with honey and banana slices stirred in. They glanced excitedly at each other over the rims of their bowls, obviously bursting to say something. Rietta's parents sat at the table next to them, also exchanging glances at the girls' strange behaviour and obvious excitement, pleased that they seemed so happy and enthusiastic about starting another day.

Chapter Three

Dream-sharing

"I had the most amazing dream!" said Rietta, and at the same time Carla was saying, "I had a wonderful dream!" They both flung themselves onto Rietta's bed and as they bounced up into sitting positions they both said, "and you were there, too!"

They leant in closer beaming with excitement, "I knew it –" gasped Rietta, "– we both had the same dream! That's just so, so… it really is so!"

Carla was instantly serious, "I don't think it was just a dream…"

"Could it be real magic?" Rietta had taken up a cuddly, soft toy from her pillow, clutching it under her chin in both hands. It was a patchy brown and grey dog, which had once been brown and white.

"Fairy magic!" Carla smiled widely again, "I knew it!"

"Could our dreams really be… real in some way? Did we really have the same dream?"

"I know we did! You tell me yours."

"Well…" Rietta was not sure where to start, because she was not really sure where or when the dream had started, "I was out at the tree and I saw lights –"

"Fairy lights!"

Then they both spoke, as good friends who know each other very well will often speak: with their words tumbling over one another's, one friend beginning their next sentence before the other has finished, or talking at the same time, listening as they talk, talking as they listen and almost knowing what each will say even as they speak… Although they had only met the day before, it already felt like they had been best friends for years and years.

"…yes! And one of the lights turned into an actual fairy, a beautiful, delicate fairy – like the most perfect doll, all glowing with her own light and she flew down onto my hand… just then, well I thought I woke up –"

"But then you saw her again," guessed Carla.

Rietta nodded, "and you saw the boy-fairy, only he was more like actual size too. And so you followed him and… somehow he carried you into –"

"Their world," Carla cut in, "where I met you and Maral… isn't it wonderful? You see, Rietta, I've had that kind of dream before – quite often –

but it's never felt so real! Usually I just see it, like through someone else's eyes… This is the first time I've actually been there talking to the fairies… and definitely the first time anyone else has been there too – someone real, I mean. I knew someday it would happen: and it was you! You were really in my dream." Her eyes were glistening.

"Our dream!" Rietta was squeezing the soft dog so tightly that his expression was distorted into one of comic disbelief, button eyes bulging and ears unevenly erect.

"Our very own special dream. And they told us…"

"What was it they said?" They were eager to recount what they remembered, aware of how dreams can just evaporate in the light of day.

"They need us," Carla simply summed up, "We have to help them…"

"Yes we need to go there again, only for real somehow, not just in a dream."

"They said they will send a guide to show us the way!"

"But how will the guide find us? It isn't going to be Maral or Bren? But they said we'd know…"

"Perhaps we need to go and find the guide! Where should we start, though?"

Both together they said, "Our tree!"

Carla giggled.

"What?" asked Rietta with a quizzical grin.

"He's cute!" Carla meant the floppy-eared cloth dog that Rietta had been cuddling.

"Oh, this is Smugly," she handed it to Carla, "I've had him forever – supposed to have been 'snuggly', but I couldn't say it right. So, 'Smugly' stuck!"

Carla touched the black velvet snout to her own nose and said, "Please to meet you. Smugly!"

Outside, the morning mist was lifting from the slopes. The sky was deepening its colour from pale grey to blue as the hazy sun rose higher and brighter to set the drifting clouds aglow. Excited songbirds chirped as the two girls crossed the little stream and ran into the shade of the great oak, setting a few ragged crows to flight from amongst its branches, their disgruntled cawing startlingly loud in the thin morning air.

The girls were intending to start their search at the big flat-topped stone where they had laid out twigs in the pattern of their combined initials. As they circled the wide, craggy trunk for the second time, it was clear that the huge rock was, simply, no longer there. In the place where they remembered the huge stone had been, there was nothing but bare earth, squiggled with worm channels. There were no other signs of movement around it. The grass stood beaded with droplets from the light rain of the night and the early morning mists. The only footprints that disrupted this silvering of dew were their own.

Rietta stared at the empty space, "Where could it have gone?"

"Too heavy for anyone to carry…" Carla looked around at the grassland, "There are no tyre tracks."

"Who could have moved it? Or did we dream that part, too?"

"Perhaps we did… but no – here's the place where it was. There was obviously something very heavy and the right shape, right here!"

Rietta bent down and picked up something from the ground, "Look, these are our twigs."

"So, it wasn't just part of the dream." Carla concluded.

"But it was solid rock," said Rietta incredulously, bending down with hands on knees for a closer look at the space where the boulder should be, "– couldn't just disappear into thin air," she said from behind the pale veil of her hair.

"It has. Just gone."

There was a sound of movement nearby, which they would have dismissed as grazing sheep, if there had been any sheep close by.

"What was that?" Rietta's voice was an urgent whisper.

"Don't know," Carla shrugged, her dark eyes meeting Rietta's, "Could it be… the guide?"

Rietta simply replied with a meaningful look and they both set off in the direction of the sound. The path ran alongside the stream and would lead them towards the head of the valley where it disappeared into a dense thicket of woodland nestled at the foot of the steeper slopes that rose upward to either side to form the mountain pass. They could see the line of the road rising higher above the trees. A delivery van, toy-sized at this distance, laboured up the steep curve through rugged landscape where wind and grazing sheep kept the dull grass clipped and made the few tenacious trees grow all twisted and stunted. Beams of golden sunlight broke through the cloud cover and swept across the slope like searchlights, throwing the contours of the land into clear relief, picking out tiny bright white dots that were sheep and glinting harshly from the windows of the delivery van.

The village ended at the margin of the woodland, with the old post office and the medieval stone bridge that used to be the only route into the valley before they built what was still referred to as, 'the new road', by the locals.

At the point where the path ran alongside the stream and disappeared into the woodland, there was a suggestion of movement. A small dark shape moving deeper amongst the tree shadows.

"Did you see that?" Carla paused and pointed.

"I think so," confirmed Rietta, "– was it an animal, or someone small?"

"I don't know. I thought it moved like a person… Should we follow them?"

Rietta looked back at the village, its haphazard rows of cottages arranged sparsely on the gentler slopes. Entering the woods would take her out of sight of her own home. She should really let her mother know, but if she took the time to run back, they would have no chance of finding whoever, or whatever, they had just seen.

Carla sensed her apprehension, "What if it's a lost child?" she reasoned.

Rietta nodded, "The river… and the banks get pretty steep and slippery."

"OK." Carla took a deep breath, "Shall we…"

Rietta agreed by finishing the sentence, "…check it out?"

Chapter Four

A Stray in the Woods

The trees around the large oak had been felled centuries ago to clear land for the original settlement and since then, goats, and later sheep, had eaten any tender new saplings as they appear. The oak had been spared initially because it provided shelter, and acorns for pigs and as a landmark that was visible from all approaches.

The path led them away from this ancient landmark, along the side of the 'river', which at this point was a broad shallow stream, but as they neared the woods, it became increasingly fast flowing, bubbling over granite rubble and frothing white between great moss-topped boulders. They had to climb over a wood step stile and the ground on the other side, which had not been cropped by the regular grazing of sheep, was thick with bracken and bramble. The only clear way was the uneven rocky path siding the stream that took them into the shade of overhanging sessile oaks.

They picked their way slowly, taking care on the rocks and patchy grasses which were still slippery with the damp of morning, yet soon they were deep in the woods.

They made their way through the woodland. Again, they caught a glimpse of movement ahead of them, between two old and twisting trunks. This time they made it out to be a small, squat figure, dressed in dark, shapeless rags. It was moving away from them, disappearing into the shadows.

"You saw that?" asked Carla, "Could it be…?"

"Think it looked smaller than us…" whispered Rietta, "It could be…"

"A fairy?"

"The guide?"

Carla nodded, but said, "Or maybe just a lost child."

"Don't you think it seemed too, tatty, to be a fairy?" asked Rietta.

"Yes. It looked more like – I don't know –" the apprehension she felt made her voice catch, "I didn't really like the look of it."

Then they heard heavy movement from its direction, like someone running headlong through dead branches and snapping fallen twigs underfoot. They began their pursuit again, at increased pace, despite their trepidation, pausing only to listen out when they realised the sound of the movements ahead had ceased.

"Well," Carla stood with hands on hips, breathing quickly, "They've outrun us."

"Or just staying still – hiding," suggested Rietta.

"Watching."

Rietta nodded, "You mean checking us out, making sure we're the right ones?"

"That's if it was the guide, but then, why would they run away?"

"Maral and Bren said we would know the guide…"

"Well, I certainly don't know who that was."

"But – no, me neither," agreed Rietta, "But they, well they weren't your usual person, were they?"

"It could just be a child, lost and frightened in the woods."

They studied each other's faces for a moment, acknowledging that they too were a little frightened. "Then we have to help them, don't we," reasoned Rietta.

"Of course – there! Over there!"

Rietta looked where Carla had pointed and saw it again. A face. A wide, pale, almost grey face, only just discernible in the shadow of a large hood. It was smaller than they were and would have perhaps stood elbow height to them. In the subdued light, they could only just make out its clothes to be heavy and shapeless, thick with grime. It was clearly looking straight at them and what they could see of its face was contorted into an expression of fear, or anger. There was something so strange about it that sent a chill through both girls, from their scalps right down their spines. They only saw it for a moment before it turned and stumbled away.

"No, wait!" Rietta called out…

"After it!" said Carla, sounding braver than she felt.

As they half ran, half clambered, over rocks and through undergrowth, they heard a strange cry that could have been the unfamiliar call of a bird, or an exclamation of shock from a startled child. It was followed by a crashing, tumbling sound as if someone had slipped and fallen down a slope… a slope that could only lead to… the river. The clamour ended in a wet sound, like something rolling and flailing into water. The noise of birds flapping and screeching punctuated the quiet that followed.

They continued in the direction of the sound, their fear now overcome by a shared sense of panic. A child may have slipped and fallen into the river because they had startled it. They knew the river was not deep, but it was fast flowing and posed a serious, life-threatening danger. Especially to a smaller person.

They clambered down the steep bank to where the water ran white over and between the rocks of its rugged bed. They scanned the watercourse in both directions, but there was no sign of child, nor creature. The water was not deep enough to entirely conceal anyone, and there were plenty of boulders with fallen branches wedged between them to cling to. It could not have swept anyone away so quickly. They split up and went either direction along the banks, looking for any signs. After several minutes, they made their ways back to each other.

"Nothing?" asked Carla.

"Nothing…" replied Rietta.

"Could it have just dislodged a rock from higher up," Carla suggested, "– and that's what we heard roll down the hill into the river? It could have gotten well away while we've been down here."

Rietta shrugged, her eyes still scanning their surroundings, "Well whatever it was, it's either run away, or has hidden very well and probably doesn't want to be found…"

"It couldn't be our guide, then…" Carla reasoned.

"Maybe it was trying to guide us. Maybe they just don't speak our language or understand that we couldn't follow that fast…"

"More than likely it was just some little kid, probably well on his way home by now."

"But, did you see his face?" asked Rietta.

"I did," Carla nodded emphatically, "– there was something really odd about it, wasn't there."

"Gave me the willies, for sure," Rietta agreed.

"It was like a really old face on a small child…"

"There was something a bit creepy about it –"

"Just a bit!" Carla agreed.

"– really old, dirty coat…"

"Could it have been a down-and-out, you know, like a tramp?" suggested Carla, "Do you have tramps in the countryside?"

"You mean a dwarf tramp in the woods?"

"I think it was something even stranger…" explained Carla, "The more I think about it, the more I think that it wasn't, really, well not quite…"

Rietta finished her sentence for her, "Not quite human?"

Carla nodded.

"It could be the guide, then?" The questioning tone indicated that Rietta was unsure of the conclusion.

"I don't know." Conceded Carla, "But we should just tell someone, though, in case they do really need some help."

"Yes." Rietta agreed, "But what would we say? We think we saw a weird lost-child-tramp-dwarf… thing…"

…and they laughed at this, despite how serious the situation might be.

"We should go up to the road," Rietta indicated the direction with a nod, "It would be the quickest way back to town and we might even see them on the way."

It was agreed, so they made their way upward along uneven paths towards the road that ran along the top of a retaining wall at the head of the valley. As they sighted the random stone blocks of the wall through the trees, they heard another strange sound. It was close-by and carried a pitiful despairing tone, more animal than human.

"It came from over there…" Carla raised a hand to indicate a tumbling patch of brambles, clogging the steep ground at the base of the wall.

"I'll go and have a look," volunteered Rietta, and started to make her way up the slope.

"Alright." Agreed Carla, starting to follow her friend.

"No, you stay here, and go for help if I get stuck, or fall, or something."

"Take care!" urged Carla.

"I will," Rietta assured her, "– I'm used to this place, lived here longer than you."

She carefully picked her way through brambles by stepping from stone to moss tump, sometimes using her hands to steady herself, or moving on all fours up the slope. First, all she could make out amongst the undergrowth was a dull brown shape, like a sack that might have fallen from a truck on the road above. When she stood up properly and took a few more steps closer, it was easy to see what it really was. A dog of medium size, wiry brown fur, damp, matted with mud and blood. It was sprawled on its right flank. Rietta could see a nasty injury above its left eye that had also torn its ear, and a long gash in its side from shoulder to haunch. One of its front legs was caked in dark stuff, twisted and appeared to be broken. There were small cuts and scratches all over where it had either struggled or fallen through the briars.

From the path, Carla could tell that Rietta had found something that caused her to halt with an apprehensive stance, she called out, "What is it?"

"Dead dog."

"Careful…" warned Carla, "Might not be dead."

Rietta moved a few steps closer, looking intently at the dog's body, then called back, "It is alive – still breathing. We're going to need a trolley or something…"

Its eyes opened. She crouched down and reached out a hand to touch it, but it bared its yellowed teeth and made a low rumbling growl. "We've got a wheelbarrow..." Rietta thought aloud.

"What?" called Carla, not quite hearing.

"Go and get the wheelbarrow," shouted Rietta, "– ask Mum."

"I'll go for a wheelbarrow..." Carla confirmed, "You stay there."

"Of course I'll stay here," said Rietta, more to the dog than to her friend who was already trotting away through the trees as fast as she could without tripping over rocks or slipping on the exposed tree roots.

A few flies were buzzing around the injured animal, one landed on the filthy fur near to the torn ear, Rietta flicked it quickly away. The dog was no longer baring its impressive teeth and, she may have imagined it, but she thought the twitch in its tail might have been a wag – the beginnings of trust. It blinked at her twice, then on the third blink the eyes remained closed. Rietta held her breath until she saw the dog's flank continue to rise and fall with its own breathing.

Partly to steady herself and partly to offer comfort, she reached out and after a moment taken to find the least cruddy patch of flank, placed her hand flat upon it. The muscles beneath the bedraggled fur twitched instantly, but then accepted the gentle contact. With her other hand, she picked a leaf off a nearby fern and used it to keep the gathering flies at bay.

She squatted like that for what seemed to be a long while. Repeatedly, she looked about, convinced that she had heard the noise of someone approaching through the undergrowth, to find no one in sight. There were frequent rustles in the treetops, like large birds rattling the branches, yet she saw no birds. More than once she thought she caught sight of movement in the shadows, movement that ceased as soon as she looked straight at it. Perhaps it was just the wind, or her own mind… it was the first time she had been alone this deep in the woods. "You're not actually alone…" she whispered, not sure if she was reassuring herself or the injured animal sprawled before her.

Eventually, she heard noises that were definitely of human origin: Carla's voice, giving directions in an excited and urgent tone, the rhythmic squeal of a single wheel, the crunching of feet on the path.

Chapter Five
A Dog's Life

When Rietta's father, Henry, came home that evening, he brought the vet along with him. She had been visiting a farm across the valley and took time out to come and see the dog. It was in the living room lying on an old piece of thick cloth that has once covered a big garden parasol. A cereal bowl of fresh water was placed nearby. Although it was a warm day outside, the inglenook stove was lit to keep the sick animal cosy. Apart from the shallow rise and fall of his ribs and an occasional twitch, he had not moved or shown any signs of life since they had painstakingly, and painfully, rolled him onto the wheelbarrow and trundled his limp body over the rough, jolting paths, taking a longer route back to the house that avoided the step stile.

The vet was a solidly built woman, probably about the same age as Rietta's parents, with dusty blonde hair pinned up to keep it off her kindly face. After a cursory examination, the vet shook her head and opened her black leather bag, taking out a syringe and a small vial. She noticed the girls watching intently and caught the father's subtle signal. Then replaced the vial and drew out another, and another. She used the hypodermic syringe to draw up the contents of both the tiny bottles.

"I'm going to give him a little jab," she explained with a gentle voice, "It will take away any pain and help him sleep right through the night – it also has medicine to stop any infection and help the swelling to go down…"

Carla nodded and Rietta asked, "Shall we bath him?"

"Not now – leave him completely alone for tonight…" the vet knelt at the dog's side to administer the injection, "If he makes it through the night, he may have a good chance of getting better." She stood up and looked very seriously at the girls, "But be prepared for the worst – he is very ill."

The girls looked back with pleading eyes as if the vet could magically make it otherwise, she smiled, "You girls have already done all you can for him – and now he is somewhere warm with people who care – and that's the best medicine there is." She turned her attention to Rietta's parents, "It's great to see young people who care about animals this much – you all did a great job." She offered a card, "Could you phone the practise in the morning and give us an update?"

Sally said, "Thank you," took the card and set it down by the telephone.

As Henry saw the vet to the door, she was saying, "That's all I can do for now. He's not in good shape at all. I don't think -" she seemed to catch herself, aware that the girls might still be listening, "- but we can't be sure until the swelling goes down and we can move him to the surgery… to get some x-rays. I'll swing by tomorrow afternoon and see how things are…"

As Henry was seeing the vet out, the girls sat on the floor next to the sleeping dog and conversed seriously, in hushed tones. As Sally joined them, crouching close by, they turned to her, it was clear from Rietta's eyes that she and Carla had decided on a question to ask.

Guessing what the question would be, Sally said, "Carla, you're welcome to stay for tea…"

Both the girls' faces lost a little of their sadness at this suggestion, "…and," Sally added, "if it's alright with your parents, you can sleepover tonight."

Rietta took hold of Carla's hands in hers and beamed, "Please stay – if you can that is – can you phone your Mum?"

"No," Carla smiled too, though there still seemed to be a tinge of sadness to her glistening dark eyes, "I cannot phone my Mum or Dad…" Rietta's smile was replaced with a quizzical frown, so Carla explained, "I live with my Aunty."

So, arrangements were made, Aunty was phoned and approved Carla's sleepover. Sally and Henry put together a quick dinner and they ate plentiful pasta in a tuna and tomato sauce. Whilst her parents were clearing up the dinner things, Rietta asked Carla where her parents were. Carla said she had never known her mother and father because they had died when she was a baby, "I was raised by my grandma in London, but she was getting too old and had to move to a home…"

"Weren't you already living at her home?" They were both speaking quietly so as not to disturb the dog resting on his make-shift bed.

"Yes, a flat… but she had to go to a special home, so people can make sure she stays safe and they can help her with shopping and meals and things like that. I had been helping, best I could, but some things I couldn't do. So, I have come here to live with my aunty. I wanted grandma to come too, but she likes being in London, it's what she's used to…"

Carla looked a little sad whilst recounting all of this, so Rietta wanted to change the subject. They were already worried enough about the injured dog without bringing up any sad memories.

Rietta fetched her sketch pad from her room and some paper for Carla to use and they shared colouring pencils, exchanged drawing tips. Rietta often drew using charcoal, but Carla had never tried and could not help smudging the lines, so Rietta showed her how to use the smudges to create shadow and give shapes better form… They drew fairies, something they had both practiced before. They drew dogs, with varying success. They tried to draw portraits of each other and laughed, not unkindly, at the results.

When it was getting late, Rietta's parents helped the girls move the table aside and take the couch apart so that the cushions could be laid out on the floor. One girl could sleep on the sofa base, and the other could use the cushions as a bed. Carla borrowed one of Rietta's nightshirts, choosing one with a friendly, big-eyed owl printed on its front.

They sat up with their camping sleeping bags wrapped around and talked until their whispers were the only sound in the cottage, except for the continuous sigh of air through the stove as it threw out golden firelight and warmth into the small square living room. Their minds were full of fairies and dogs …and what might happen tomorrow …or the next day, but their eyes desperately wanted to close and so, eventually, they had little choice but to lay back and welcome a deep dream-filled slumber.

Their dreams were of woods and dogs and sometimes of something strange, just at the corner of their vision, which turned into something else when they looked at it. No fairies came to them that night, though the next morning something that seemed almost miraculous happened...

Chapter Six

The Name Game

During the night, shortly after the two girls finally fell asleep, the dog's head raised from the bundle of duvet that Rietta had kindly formed into a sort of pillow and looked around the room, blinking, taking in its surroundings. The stove was burning very low at this time, casting a dull orange glow over the walls that was reflected in the sheen of the dog's eyes and tinted the tongue as it lolled out over the impressive teeth that also gleamed. The animal's fur was so filthy and matted that no other part could catch the light and it appeared to be a large moving shadow as it attempted to stand. After much effort, the injured front leg buckled under the weight and it sank back down, panting heavily. Then tried again almost immediately. It was a struggle to lift first its elbows off the duvet and then to rise to its full height at the shoulders, and of equal effort to raise its hindquarters until, finally, it stood. It surveyed the room until the shining eyes fixed on the two girls.

As the dog took a tentative step from its makeshift bed there was a slight creaking of floorboards. At this, Rietta moved slightly in her sleep and an array of expressions flitted across her face, a suggestion of a smile that dissolved into a soft frown and then to the face of someone peacefully sleeping once more. The dog took another step closer… and another… closer… until the jaws hung almost directly above Rietta's head. Its breath was ragged and rasping with the exertion of simply walking those few feet across the room. It looked down at her as she slept, her skin and hair pale against the pillow. The dog closed its jaws so now only the eyes shone like jewels, just inches from Rietta's sleeping face. With nostrils flaring it explored the scents of the girls and carefully studied their sleeping faces… as if considering whether they were his jailers or his saviours.

It stood like this for a long while, then smacked its lips and began panting again. With continuing effort, he moved to the bowl of water and took a good long drink. The sound of lapping and splashing was loud in the quiet of the early hours, but the girls slept on. Then, painfully, he returned to the bundled duvet near the dying stove where he laid down carefully and quickly descended back into his own sleep of twitching, troubled dreams.

As the last warm glow of the stove faded, the first cool light of morning was creeping in through the window. Rietta awoke first and immediately rolled off her bed of sofa cushions and moved across the room on all fours, like a dog herself. She studied the animal form very seriously until she was sure that the grubby flanks were rising and falling with even breath.

"It's alive!" she whispered through her smile, "Still alive…"

Carla was now awake and stumbled over the sofa cushions, tripping on one and only just catching her balance again. She knelt down next to Rietta saying, "The vet said that if you lived through the night you may be OK!" and at this, even though the dog's eyes remained closed, the tail wagged, feebly at first and then a few vigorous whacks into the duvet: thump, thump, thump.

The girls laughed and very softly put their hands onto fur that was still spiky with dried grime. The dog's toffee coloured eyes opened and it raised its head in an attempt to smell them. Together, they offered their hands and the dog inspected each for a moment before gently lapping at their fingers with a big pink tongue.

They sat quietly with the dog as the day outside brightened and the last glimmer of orange warmth left the door of the stove as the sun rose from behind the mountains and sent a shaft of morning gold through the window. The dog also rose and, tentatively testing its legs, went slowly over to its water bowl. The girls watched, smiling at each other, but not wanting to speak in case they distracted the dog from his mission. It had a short noisy drink and then sat awkwardly by the bowl looking at them expectantly.

"I think he wants breakfast!" said Rietta.

Carla nodded and asked, "What have you got?"

"Biscuits." The dog seemed to sit up straighter at this.

"Perhaps," suggested Carla, "We should check with the vet first?"

"And, we have to name him, too. He can't have a breakfast before a name!"

"He's an old dog, y'know, probably already has a name…"

They both looked him over for a while, then Rietta made the first guess, "Fido!" The dog's good ear perked up and the other fluttered limply.

"Bonzo?" coaxed Carla and he cocked his head to one side, a bemused snaggle upon his snout.

They then took it in turns to think of names that suited and say them as enticingly as possible, watching for any flicker of recognition in his eyes or posture:

"Max," guessed Rietta.

"Rex," suggested Carla.

"Barnie!"

"Aluiscious?"

"Scooby."

"Sam?"

"Samson!"

"He looks like he'd be strong," agreed Carla, "Hercules..."

"Zeus?"

The girls could not help but giggle at his quizzical expressions as he seemed to struggle to make sense of this tirade of abstract sounds…

"Apollo," continued Carla.

"Hey, there, Chief!" ventured Rietta.

"Prince."

"Captain."

"– Kirk."

"Do you think he's a clever dog?" pondered Rietta, "How about, Sherlock?"

"Elementary, my dear *Watson*?"

"Happy!"

"Mojo."

He stood and took a few steps closer before plonking down heavily again, this time looking even more comical, with his jaws slack and his tongue lolling. The stiff, unkempt fur stuck out in random tufts.

"Dave," Rietta said with an air of familiarity.

"Caesar," Carla announced with grandeur.

"Duke."

"How'd you do, Hal?"

"Alfonse."

"Ah, Jim-lad."

"Jolly!"

"Jeff?"

"Scrufty –"

Woof! A short, sharp bark resounded through the cottage. The tail thumped the floorboards.

"Scrufty!" The girls said together and giggled as he loped across to them and lowered his head in range of their outstretched hands.

The bark must have woken Rietta's parents because as they ruffled the thick grimy fur of the dog's neck and scratched behind his one good ear, they heard the flooring creak upstairs and the distinctive squeak of the bathroom door.

Rietta and Carla were both so bursting with excitement that not only was the dog still alive, but he seemed fairly full of life. So when Sally, Rietta's mother, announced she was going to phone the vet, both girls wanted to be the one to pass on the good news. Luckily, the phone had a 'speaker' function.

The vet sounded very surprised that the dog had recovered enough to eat. She advised offering Scrufty a light breakfast and after some discussion a small bowl of sardines and rye crackers was prepared. The bowl was placed near to his make-shift bed and at first he stretched out his neck sniffed at it eyeing them both, warily, before licking at the food. He then pulled himself to his feet eagerly, and noisily, devouring it. As they watched him eat, they exchanged speculations on where the dog may have come from. Rietta did not recognise him as a local dog and they decided he must have fallen – or been intentionally flung – from a moving car on the road above where they had found him.

"Who could do such a thing?" wondered Rietta.

"Some people," said Carla, "are simply horrid – don't care a bit about animals."

"I think animals are people, just like human people…"

"But some humans are so much worse than animals!"

"Even, evil."

"Evil, even!" they said together and giggled because they had thought of the same silly wordplay to lighten the conversation and cheer themselves up. Besides, it is easy to smile when watching a dog enjoy its breakfast.

After lunch, the vet visited to give Scrufty a more thorough looking over. She ran her hands over his body, feeling for any swellings and checking the bone structure beneath. For most of the examination his tale wagged. It only stopped swinging when she felt around his injured ear. When she attempted to flex his injured foreleg, a low rumbling growl came from deep in his chest. He seemed to be studying her face intently. There was the merest glimpse of teeth as his lips tightened, but he made no move to bite – he understood that these people were helping him.

Throughout the examination, the vet gently and confidently continued, not at all put off by his grumblings. When she had finished, she stood up with a smile on her face, and said, "Are you sure this is the same dog?"

The girls simply returned her smile and Henry asked, "Does it look like good news, then?"

The vet nodded, "Miraculous! I didn't really think there was much hope, but the injuries…" she shrugged, "…must have looked a lot more serious than they actually were. I'm still not sure about the foreleg, not broken but there might be a tiny fracture… apart from that, it's all surface damage. Nothing more than cuts and bruises."

She explained that he would move stiffly for the next few days and instructed the girls to keep a close eye on his walk: if he was not placing his weight on the injured leg by the end of the week, they were to bring him in to the surgery for x-rays. Before she left, she gave Scrufty another jab, to help with pain and swelling, and said again how surprised she was at the quickness of his recovery. She chuckled and scruffled Scrufty's head saying, "I might have to write this one up for the journals!" Then, as she gathered her kit together she said, "Actually, girls, that would be a really helpful thing you could do for me…"

"What?" asked Rietta eagerly.

"…keep a record of how he does. Make notes about how active he is every day, how much he eats, how much he sleeps, when he does anything of note, what mischief he gets up to… Treat it like a summer-school project."

"You mean," Carla grinned, "Keep a dog-log!"

Rietta giggled at this and said, "We'd love to do that!"

"And," added the vet encouragingly, "You must let me see your findings in a few weeks' time – before the end of the summer hols?"

Chapter Seven

Recuperation

For the first few, slow days of his recovery, Scrufty never ventured far from his duvet by the stove. The persistent rains tended to seep into the walls of the stone cottage and chill the air, so the little stove was kept constantly aglow to help drive out any damp.

The two girls never ventured far from Scrufty. To begin with, their entries in the dog-log were short and repetitive, mainly recording what he ate each day. Most evenings, Carla stayed for dinner. Sometimes they would fall asleep together, whilst drawing in Rietta's room and Sally would make a quick phone call to Carla's aunty to let her know of impromptu sleepovers. Her Aunty worked very unsociable hours as a care nurse, so was more than happy to know that Carla was amongst friends and being looked after properly.

This time the girls spent together, and the shared responsibility of supervising Scrufty's recovery, firmed their friendship just as if they had known each other for years instead of a matter of days. During an unseasonal rainy period, they were usually sat at the dining room table so they could keep an eye out for signals that meant Scrufty needed to visit the garden. Usually between showers, he would limp out to do what a dog must do. A red plastic raincoat was hung next to the kitchen door so one of the girls could accompany him and clean up after. They dutifully took turns. A towel was also kept handy to dry off the dog with playful scruffling and in this way, most of the caked-in mud and dirt transferred from fur to towel.

Those rainy days were none-the-less bright, with rainbows or glittering curtains of backlit rain. It never got too cold, so when Scrufty seemed to be walking without discomfort, they decided it was time to try a proper bath and finally find out what colour he really was.

They donned plastic kagools over their brightly coloured summer shorts and T-shirts, Rietta in the red one and Carla in blue, then prepared a row of several buckets along the garden path and filled them with kettles of warm water. While his fur was already dampened by a downpour they managed to squirt him with some baby shampoo and, taking care to avoid his injuries, worked up a foam before he seemed to know what they were planning. In fact, he seemed to enjoy the attention and cooperated to begin with, until he decided it was a game of 'let's all share the lather?'

The warm water in buckets was intended for rinsing. "I'll keep him busy," Rietta volunteered, "While you pour over the rinse water…" Not as simple as it sounded, for Scrufty was becoming increasingly active and excited by the new game and presented a moving target. The half-full bucket was a bit heavy for Carla to manoeuvre with any accuracy and, although she was aiming at Scrufty as she tipped it, most of the water poured over Rietta's head. "Oh, no! So, sorry!" Carla managed to gasp between guffaws.

"Right," said Rietta, using both hands to drag the clinging curtains of wet hair from across her eyes, "My turn to do some rinsing!" There was mock menace in her tone. The girls took turns with the buckets until they were both well and truly soaked, their kagools holding in the wet rather than keeping it out. Somehow, they had also managed to rinse Scrufty, who was barking and splattering through the broad puddle of muddy water that they had made. Then it began to rain heavily in another torrent of warm, fat, splashy drops. All three were already too wet to mind.

"Well," Rietta laughed, "That's something to write-up in the dog-log!"

It turned out that Scrufty was a gingery, golden brown, with paler, almost white chest and underbelly.

By the time the weather brightened again and started to resemble a real summer once more, Scrufty could walk just fine. They shared some lovely lazy afternoons in the shade of their special tree. The girls sketched the landscape, each other and Scrufty, when he would keep still.

He seemed to develop a fascination with sniffing around the imprint left by the big boulder. Rietta showed Carla how to finger-knit simple plaits from reeds and long stems of grass and then how to weave them into circles and star shapes. As they were hanging these from the lower branches, creating a 'fairy bower' for themselves, Scrufty padded about in the shade, back and forth between the patch of bare earth and each girl, in turn. When Rietta looked down, she saw that he had gathered a little pile of sticks and twigs at her feet and was now sat a short distance away, watching expectantly, tail gently swishing to and fro through the grass.

"Hah!" said Rietta, "Looks like he wants to play fetch…" she bent and picked up the weightiest stick and tossed it out into the sunshine. Scrufty watched it fly through the air and then padded over to retrieve it, dropping it back onto the pile at her feet. Rietta was pleased to note that his limp had all but vanished. This time she threw the stick a little further, she shouted, "Fetch!" Scrufty calmly retrieved it again.

She smiled over her shoulder at Carla, who was crouching down to inspect the little pile of sticks that Scrufty had brought to her. She looked up with a strange expression on her face, squinting a little at the brightness beyond where Rietta stood. "Rietta?" she said quietly.

"What is it?"

"These sticks… look at the sticks he brought to you."

Rietta glanced down at her feet, "What about them?" Then she also crouched down to take a closer look, and began fingering the twigs and sorting them into a pattern. "These sticks…" she glanced up at Scrufty and then to Carla again, "They're the same ones…"

Carla nodded, "These are the exact same sticks I used to lay out my initials."

"And these are mine!" Rietta grinned up at Scrufty who was watching with his head tilted to one side as if expecting some sort of reward. "Good boy," she said, then in a quieter voice, more to Carla, "How did you know?"

The girls sorted and rearranged the sticks together to form the recognisable pattern of their combined initials. They were all there. Scrufty had found every stick and twig they had used and brought the right ones to each girl. They both looked at the dog with wonderment.

"He must have been able to tell by the smell…" Rietta suggested, not sounding entirely convinced.

Carla nodded, "Perhaps he was some sort of a tracker dog?"

The next day was the warmest and brightest yet. It seemed to the girls that summer had finally arrived and thrown its glorious gown of green and sky blue across the valley. Butterflies awoke and flitter-flashed their colours among the heather and daisies. Bees buzzed all the more loudly and birds sang with renewed vigour.

Scrufty seemed full of energy and eagerly joined in with a game of tag. He chased the girls in circles around the tree and they laughed when they nearly tripped over him or collided with each other. They stopped when they were too short of breath to carry on and leaned against the ancient trunk while Scrufty looked at them, tongue lolling as he panted heavily in the heat. They took him over to the stream to remind him to have a drink and so he did, his big pink tongue splashing away in the cool water for what seemed like a full minute, at least. Then he looked up, finally satisfied, sparkling streams of water flowing from the furry fronds of his lower jaw.

They both patted his flanks and said, "Good boy!" but then his good ear pricked up. His tail stopped wagging, his jaw tightened. His entire body had tensed and began to tremble with energy. A low rumble started deep in his chest. They felt it under their hands before they heard it. Then the rumbling moved to his throat and became a threatening growl. Instinctively, the girls took a step back exchanging glances of concern, but it was not directed towards them.

Scrufty was staring intently past them, upstream to where the brook emerged from the shady woodland. Suddenly he shot away like a fur-blurred cannon ball. In seconds, he had reached the fence that hemmed the woodland

and was throwing himself against the wire, barking and snapping at the air. By the time Rietta and Carla caught up, whatever it was that had set him off had vanished.

A little shaken by this uncharacteristic display of aggression, the girls gently patted the agitated dog, ruffling the thick fur at his shoulders. He ceased his snarling and became instantly calmer. Carla crouched down at his side and peered into the shadowed woods beyond, "What d'you think that was?" she said, breathlessly. Rietta shook her head, "I don't know," she said quietly and, despite the summer heat, shuddered as if chilled, "I think we should go back to the house."

After lunch, they spent the rest of the day, quietly and safely, in the back garden. They drank glasses of cool fruit juice, sat on folding chairs at a folding picnic table. They up-dated their dog-log for the vet and then drew fairies, using a set of day-glow pens to fill them in with rainbows of bright colour.

As she was delicately filling-in the wings with an intricate lace-like pattern, Rietta asked, "Do you think it might have been our guide?"

"Perhaps it was…" said Carla, rubbing out a leg of her fairy and trying to re-draw it to match the other one, "But I don't think there's much chance of us finding out with Scrufty on guard duty, is there?"

"Think he sensed something that was there? Something not of our world?"

Carla nodded and reached across for the scissors, "By the way he reacted to it, I'd say." She had the idea of cutting her fairy out so she could hang it from one of the bushes. Rietta did the same with hers and the light breeze moved them causing the colourful paper wings to flutter a little.

Rietta smiled and said, "You and me – as fairies!" They admired their cut-outs for a moment until Rietta said excitedly, "Hey, that gives me an idea!"

Back at the table, she took another sheet of paper and drew a dragon with its wings spread from one edge to the other, as if viewed from directly above. Then she folded it as if she was making a paper aeroplane. Carla liked that idea.

As she was showing Carla how to do the folding, Rietta said, "Don't you just wish that dragons were really real?"

"I think they must be – or must have been, once." Carla said absently, concentrating on keeping a fold nice and straight, "Every society around the world has some legend about a dragon, or something like…" she looked up at the craggy mountain sides surrounding the green valley, "This looks just the place they would have lived."

"Perhaps they did…" nodded Rietta thoughtfully, "Perhaps they still do, in a way, up here," she reached across and gently tapped Carla's forehead with a finger.

"Then we have both given them a home…" Carla smiled.

"And," added Rietta, "Maybe, we can release them back into the wild, one day!" She illustrated this by sending her paper-dragon-plane into a long curving arc that ended with a sudden nose-dive onto the lawn a few feet from Scrufty, who sniffed at it with little interest.

"Well, if fairies can be real in dreams…" Carla launched hers and it glided up high, stalled and stooped into a smooth curve that ended up in the shrubbery, "…then so can dragons!"

"Do you think we'll see them? When the guide takes us through to the fairy lands?" Rietta retrieved her dragon and was un-crumpling its head.

Carla shrugged, "Do you think the guide will ever show up?"

"Do you think it is anything more than a dream?"

"A dream we both had!" Carla reminded her emphatically, "Our special dream."

"Mmm…" Rietta was thoughtfully inspecting her paper model, "I want to see one, really-for-real… I want to ride on a dragon's back."

Carla smiled and nodded. She relaunched her dragon-plane and as she watched it glide said, "Not all dragons are friendly, though. In storybooks, they also eat people – especially princesses and young girls – and burn down villages."

"Oh yes, well…" Rietta grinned, "I'd rather not meet one of those for real!"

They drew and coloured-in more paper dragons, experimenting with cutting the wings into better shapes. They tried different folds and designs to see which ones flew the best. Scrufty showed a passing interest and half-heartedly chased them on the first few flights, but soon became content to lay down in the shade of the house. He rested his fuzzy chin on his forepaws, just watching, occasionally giving a few lazy wags of his tail.

Chapter Eight

A Visit to Grandma's

It was a fine day and Scrufty was restlessly padding around the house and trotting up and down the garden path. His eyes were bright, his tail wagging and tongue lolling. Carla and Rietta agreed that he was ready for a proper walk and so Rietta decided they should take him for a visit to her Nanna's, because it was not too far and they could let the dog rest there a while before they headed back.

"With any luck," Rietta said as she clipped Scrufty's new lead to his new collar, "Nan'll tell us one of her fairy stories. She knows lots of good ones."

The dog walked calmly ahead of the girls, only pulling occasionally in his eagerness to venture further, regularly glancing back as if to check they were still following. Taking a route from Rietta's back gate, they walked alongside the stream and found that it had conveniently washed away some of the bank, eroding a gap under the fence that they could all duck through to avoid having to heft Scrufty over the step-stile.

They followed the path through the woodland, enjoying its cool shade. Scrufty walked with his snout down, zig-zagging across the track, snorting at the leaf litter. He paused with his head almost disappearing into a hollow between mossy tree roots, tail swaying high in the air.

Rietta crouched at his shoulders, "What you found, boy?"

At her side, Carla said, "I always think those holes under roots are fairy doorways…"

"Or like skylights," suggested Rietta, "to an underground hall where they hold their banquets."

Scrufty snorted, withdrew his head and, finding the girls down at his level, flapped a soily tongue at their faces, catching Rietta across the chin.

"Eugh!" she said with a big smile and quickly stood up out of range, and wiping her sleeve across her chin added, "Probably just where some squirrel hordes her nuts…"

Carla clapped her hands together and said, "Squirrels!"

Scrufty answered with a short, sharp bark and then something rustled a short distance away amongst the bramble and bracken. His focus instantly turned in the direction of the sound with ear up and snout raised, nostrils flared as he scented the air. His tail ceased its wagging, for the first time since they had left the house. Shoulders tensed and he suddenly strained forth against the lead, almost pulling it from Rietta's grasp, until Carla caught hold of it as well. A deep rumble escaped from his throat and the long muzzle ridged up as he bared his teeth.

"What is it!" gasped Rietta, both girls leaning back to restrain the dog. They peered in the direction of his aggression and saw something move. A squat and grey thing seemed to be watching them from the undergrowth. It was just a glimpse as the dappled shadows danced before a breezy gust. Then, as the foliage became still again it seemed to be gone.

Carla spoke in a voice that was intended to be reassuring, though wavered a little too much,

"It's OK, Scrufty… nothing there to worry about…"

The growling subsided and Rietta also tried a calming voice, "It's nothing but a rock…" Then she leant in and whispered to Carla, "Do you think it was that… thing. Again?"

"Our lost-child-tramp-dwarf-guide?" Carla shrugged, "Well, whatever it was – if was anything except a squirrel – Scrufty scared it off for us. But somehow, these woods suddenly seem spooky again…"

In a level voice, Rietta said, "Shall we go up to the road, now?"

"Good plan…"

Scrufty dragged them up the wooded slope, following a curve that avoided the boulder-cluttered patch that he had been snarling at, and joined the main road at the medieval bridge. As they left the shady woods, the dog seemed to relax and return to excited tail wagging and sniffing as he went.

As they were approaching a large pebble-dash and breeze-block building, Rietta suggested they stop for quick visit to the Library. They looped Scrufty's lead through one of the bicycle stands at the side of the small, empty car-park and told him to, "sit and stay," and reassured him that they would not be long.

It was quiet and pleasantly cool inside. There were rows and rows of shelves and a few computer workstations along the rear wall. The woman behind the counter was tall and slim with short-cropped silver-grey hair and wore a featureless white blouse. The shocking pink frames of her large spectacles with long earrings to match, more than made up for the starched whiteness of her attire. The librarian smiled and greeted Rietta by name, who then politely introduced Carla.

The bicycle rack where they had left Scrufty, was right outside one of the big floor-to-ceiling windows, so people could keep an eye on their bikes. The girls could see him sitting silently to attention, peering in at them, his eyes following their every move when they came into view. Nothing would distract him. This made them feel too guilty to spend long browsing and they quickly made their choices. As Rietta was checking-out a book on dog-care and a richly illustrated volume on Welsh Folklore, she asked, "Do you have any books on fairy-dogs?"

The librarian glanced up from date-stamping the books, "I don't think we have. That's one you'll have to write…"

Scrufty welcomed them with thrashing tail as they unclipped him from his tether and, with Rietta's rucksack heavier on her shoulders with the weight of books, they continued past the Post Office. Then cut diagonally across the park, with its brightly coloured swings, seesaw and slide. The bowling lawn was super-green under the high sun. After skirting the churchyard, they headed up through a network of steep streets lined with grey, stone-fronted houses. On dull days, the town looked drab and damp. On such a bright, sunny day, with the slate roofs gleaming and the granite facades sparkling with quartz inclusions, it took on the atmosphere of a mountain town on some Mediterranean island.

Some of the houses had narrow front gardens, barely big enough to contain a shrub or tub, but most were paved-over and adorned only with stacks of plastic recycling crates and wheeled bins. Rietta paused outside one house with an overgrown trellis around its door and window, thick with huge, pink and purple clematis blooms. After ringing the front doorbell, they waited a short while, but there was no reply.

"She'll be round the back, in her garden," guessed Rietta from previous experience.

Because the house was mid-terrace, they had to walk a short distance to a narrow road between two houses a few doors down. It was only just wide enough for a car to squeeze through and took them around to a track of crumbling tarmac that ran between the back gardens of twin rows of terraced houses. At the back, most were still proudly showing off their random stone walls. A few had been pebble-dashed and the years had dulled them to the colour of a dirty beach on a dull day. A few had been freshly painted in cheerful pastel colours. Each house was backed by a long, narrow garden, some of these had been paved to make parking spaces for cars to pull up onto. Not Rietta's nan's.

They stopped at a gate that led to a garden fringed with the greenest hedges, all neatly trimmed into rolling curves that always reminded Rietta of miniature forest-covered hills. Between the hedges, a winding stone path led from the gate and disappeared into a garden crowded with flowering shrubs, roses, box-bordered flowerbeds. They could see the roof of a little hexagonal shed-cum-summer-house and above it a white-painted and rather palatial dovecote set on a tall pole.

The girls ventured through the gate, pausing to count the butterflies, feeding on a white buddleia, its branches drooping with the weight of so many blossoms. There were a number of painted-ladies and peacock butterflies, and Rietta was able to point out the rarer comma, with its ragged dusty-orange wings. There were also plenty of bees of all shapes and sizes, but they seemed to favour the pale blue rosemary flowers festooning the lower bushes at the side of the path.

There were so many flowers of so many hues that Rietta's Nan was almost camouflaged by her floral-print frock and matching sun-hat. They may well have walked straight past her if not for the bright orange gardening gloves and flash of busy pruning shears. Scrufty gave a lip-billowing woof when he noticed her, tugging on his lead and wagging his tail.

"And hello to you, too!" said Rietta's Nan, peering at them from her elevated position on a portable gardening caddy that also functioned as a step. Carla was holding Scrufty's lead and he towed her across the small patch of velvet green lawn.

"Hi, Nanna!" Rietta called cheerily from behind, "May I introduce Carla and Scrufty."

The woman stepped down onto the lawn to greet them, saying, "I presume Scrufty is the one with four legs?" She took off a glove and bent to quickly scruffle the dog's head, looked up to say, "So you must be Carla?"

Carla nodded, "Pleased to meet you," then she laughed as Scrufty managed to slap a wet lick across the lady's cheek.

"Well," she said, also with a broad smile, "I am Rietta's Nanna, but you shall call me, Ivy…"

Carla tried to bring Scrufty back under control, managing to say, "Makes sense…"

Ivy asked, "How so?" wiping the back of her hand across her cheek.

"Well – you being named after a plant…" Carla nodded to indicate their surroundings, "Because your garden is so… lush!"

"Ah, yes – thank you!" She looked over at Rietta, "If you shut the gate behind you, you can let Scrufty off – he's raring to go explore!"

Rietta nodded, so Carla unfastened the lead from his collar with a click. They all three laughed at his antics as Scrufty bounded away to run circuits around the shrubbery and check the perimeters. His good ear stood erect and alert, swivelling this way and that to catch birdsong and the thudding of music from a neighbour's open window. His snout snorted loudly under clumps of flowers as he seemed to track a scent from one side of the garden to the other, occasionally disturbing big bumble-bees that buzzed at him noisily.

Rietta smiled, "He's found something that smells good!"

"Cat, I bet…" Carla guessed.

"Or," suggested Rietta's Nanna, "Perhaps it was Albert. Doing his rounds last night," and seeing Carla's quizzical expression explained, "Albert is our friendly neighbourhood hedgehog."

The garden was long and narrow. As they walked up the stone path towards the back of the house, with its window frames painted a rosy pink, Ivy, pointed out some of the plants they passed. Most were herbs, with some sort of culinary or household use, but there was also an abundance of vibrant blooms in various tones of rainbow colour. Even the small lawns were dotted with daisy and dandelion, because, "Dandelions are clever flowers - they keep the sunshine safe for us on dull days…" The girls knew exactly what she meant, for each flower shone bright like a tiny golden sun. "…and daisies remind me of when I was a little girl myself, playing in the grass and counting ants…" Rietta knew her grandmother must have been a little girl once, but she found it hard to picture it. "I didn't even make daisy-chains then, I didn't like to pull up a thing of such simple beauty."

The garden path was bordered with lavender and rosemary. "Run your fingers through them," she instructed and as the girls ruffled them they released a heavy and warm floral aroma. "That's how all the bees find them!" said Rietta, who always thought the colour of her Nanna's eyes matched the pale purple-lilac of the small flowers.

"Yes," smiled Ivy, "Bees, butterflies and beneficial bugs can't get enough of them."

"Bees, butterflies and beneficial bugs?" giggled Rietta, "Is that a tongue twister?"

Carla quickly repeated, "Bees, butter-flies and bene-ficial bugs?" and Rietta tried to say it faster. They tried again, even faster and by the time they got to the third or fourth attempt, they were actually saying, "Beans, batteries and butterficial plugs!" Then they were both laughing too much to say anything for a moment.

Rietta's Nanna was also chuckling, her lilac eyes sparkling in the shade of her sunhat, and in the same tongue-twister staccato she added gleefully, "But, little imps and no-good-goblins can't stand the smell of 'em at all!"

When they reached the house, something hanging to one side of the back door attracted Carla's attention. She noticed a strange hollow ball, about the size of a netball, made from tightly woven branches, with a few colourful ribbons intertwined with them. She asked, "Is there normally something growing in that hanging basket?"

"Ah," Ivy reached up to touch it gently with her fingertips and said, "– that's not a hanging basket,"

Rietta added, knowingly, "It's a spirit home…"

"Spirit home?" Carla repeated the phrase as a question.

Ivy explained, "It's a little house for the garden spirits to shelter in. I made it from hazel withies, so they know they are welcome…" She led the way through the back door and into a narrow kitchen, saying, "There's another one in here…" A high shelf, lined with assorted jars of jams and pickles, spanned the kitchen window over the sink and from it hung a slightly smaller sphere, "…for the kitchen brownies to sleep in."

"So," said Carla with delight, "You do believe in fairies too!"

"My garden wouldn't be as – 'lush' – if the fairies didn't help out a bit." She smiled, "And my home baking has been much more successful since I made them feel at home! Speaking of which, how would you girls like some fresh baked bread and lemon-curd?"

"Yes, please!" they nodded, and at that moment, seemingly on cue at the mention of food, Scrufty bustled in from the garden, wide-eyed and panting with excitement, tail thudding against the antique pine of a cupboard door.

Rietta's nan threw her hands in the air as Scrufty pushed past her and headed towards the room beyond the kitchen, "But first things first!" she said and reached down a small saucepan from its hook under one of the shelves. She ran it full of water from the tap and placed it on the floor in a corner. "Scrufty!" she called brightly and the dog re-appeared to take a long splashy drink.

Rietta asked, "Would you tell us one of your fairy stories?"

Her Nanna had already rinsed her hands and was getting the bread-board and china plates out, "Of course I will," she said, "You girls go through to the living room and make sure that

Scrufty doesn't get up to any mischief whilst I make some lemonade… then we can settle down for a proper story-time."

Chapter Nine

Just One of Nanna Ivy's Fairy Stories

The girls were soon sitting comfortably in the neat little living room. A tray of snacks and drinks was laid out on the polished table-top before them, and Scrufty had settled down on the hearth rug. Carla had expected Rietta's Nanna Ivy, to bring out a book of fairy tales to read from, but instead she simply stared into the air over their heads for a few moments, chin resting lightly on the fingers of one hand, eyes unfocussed as she brought the story to mind.

Then she settled back into her favourite armchair and looked at the girls in turn before asking, "Shall I begin?"

They both said she should. So she did:

"One day, once upon a time, two little girls were out walking. They were sisters and had been gathering berries in the woods and on their way back home they saw something in the long grass. To start with it looked like an old coat with red lining. Now, a coat, in those days, was a prized possession, you would not just leave it lying around – if someone had lost it, then they would be most grateful for its return and if the owner could not be found, then it could keep you warm and cosy in the cold nights. Either way, it was something that they could not pass by. But as they went nearer to investigate, the saw that the coat was made of white fur and the red was blood. Now they became fearful thinking that they may have found the site of a terrible accident, or perhaps something even more terrible, a murder… but they soon realised that they were looking down on an injured dog. Not just any dog, mind you, but what might have been a fine hound, perhaps a nobleman's dog.

"Now, back then, it was forbidden for a peasant to talk to a nobleman, or to merely touch a nobleman's dog. If you did, you could be flogged, or put in the stocks, or even taken to the gallows hill."

Rietta asked, "What, exactly, is a 'gallows hill'?"

"Well… Remember, this story is from long ago, when the law was harsh and cruel. You could be hanged for stealing bread, even if your family were starving, so most towns had a hill where they built a gallows to hang people.

"So, if the dog had been dead, then that would have been that and they would have walked away, perhaps reporting it to the burgomaster later… but just as they turned to leave, the dog let out a whine of distress. It was not dead and it needed their help. So, they decided they had to take it back to their village and see if they could care for it and make it better. So, between them they managed to carry the heavy hound –"

"How did they manage?" Rietta wanted to know.

"We had to go and get a wheelbarrow," added Carla.

"They were peasant girls," Nanna explained, "So they were used to carrying heavy things – buckets from the well and from the milking sheds, big bundles of firewood on their backs, sacks of vegetables to the market – and that was miles away…"

"Anyway, with some difficulty, because the dog was barely alive and so it was very floppy, they managed to carry it between them – they were putting it down every so often for a rest when their muscles got tired. But they eventually got it back to their farmstead. They got some straw from the stable and made a bed out of an old crate near to their fireplace to keep it warm that night. They knew a little bit about sick animals, from growing up on their little farm, and they knew the dog may not ever wake up again…"

"In the morning, though, it was still alive and even opened its eyes. But it could do no more than that… One of the little girls ate only half her oats for breakfast and took her bowl over. She placed it an inch away from the poor doggy's nose and it just managed to lap up some of the porridge. Her sister filled her bowl with water and held that steady for the dog to take a long and much needed drink…"

Carla made a little interrupting noise and asked, "Where are their mum and dad?"

"Their parents were away for a few days, having taken the geese to market, miles away in the nearest big town – there were not any cities anywhere near, but if they were lucky, they could catch the drovers in the big town and sell their geese to be driven hundreds of miles more to the big city…"

"Driven?" Rietta smiled at her own question, "– like in a car?"

The girls giggled and Nanna Ivy chuckled, "Did you know," she asked, "that the boys who drove the geese down to London used to fill their boots with lard – pork fat?"

"Eww!" said Carla wrinkling her nose, "– why would they do that?"

Rietta answered, "So all the dogs would follow them!?"

There was more giggling and chuckling.

"Yes," Nanna Ivey chuckled too, "– that may well have been a consequence! But, can you think what the real reason was?"

Carla tried to look serious, "So, if they ran out of food they could fry their shoes?"

"No…" Nanna smiled, but did not chuckle, in case that had not been meant as a joke.

Rietta nudged Carla with an elbow and added, "Make the shoes waterproof?"

Nanna nodded, "Yes, that was one of two main reasons… the fat would make the shoes waterproof and also all squishy-squashy and slippery and, so…" She arched her brows questioningly at the girls awaiting their best guess.

Carla blurted out, "Stop them getting blisters!"

"That's right, on such a long walk with tough old leather boots that probably did not fit too well, they would get very sore feet from damp and rubbing, the fat helped against both those problems."

"As well," added Rietta with a smirk, "as helping them to make friends with all the dogs."

"Yes," Nanna conceded, "and probably that too."

Carla wanted the story to continue, "So, what about the two girls, home alone with the sick dog?"

"Well, yes, Hmm…" Nanna Ivy paused for effect, "They were very caring and made sure the dog ate little and often, had plenty of fresh water to drink, and because it could not walk, they had to clean up after it too…

"They got out their father's fishing line and managed to catch one fairly good trout, which they boiled up. You know what, even though they were hungry and would have liked to eat the fish themselves, they realised that the dog needed some good meat if it was to get better, so they carefully removed all the little bones, contenting themselves with the occasional suck of a fishy finger. And what did they do with the fish?"

Carla knew, "They gave the fish to the dog for its dinner."

Rietta had heard the story before and added a line she could recall, "– which it wolfed down with gusto!"

"Exactly what they did – yes." Nanna patted her thighs with her flat hands for emphasis, "Then, they added some turnip and onion to the water they had boiled it in and made a surprisingly tasty and nutritious soup for themselves.

"This went on for many days. They cared for the dog every spare moment, which were few and far between, because, with their parents away, they still had all the chores to do in running their farmstead. Cleaning out chicken coops, mucking out the pig, feeding all the animals, and milking the cows and the smelliest, biggest and ickiest job of all, cleaning the cattle yard and cowshed. It took them most of their days and whenever they got the chance they checked on the dog and tempted it with more and more food. In the nights, after the fire died down and it was dark, they would even lay down next to the dog to keep it warm.

"Soon the dog rewarded their hard work and kindness with a wag of the tail and a lick of the hands when they fed it… and a few days later it stood up and could walk on its own four legs to its food and water bucket…"

Carla asked, "What had they called the dog?"

"Ah, yes, a name for the dog? Mmm…" Nanna put her fingertips to her chin as if in thought, tapping her lips with a forefinger, then gestured to the girls, "Well… What would you have called the dog?"

The girls both glanced down at the relaxed dog near the hearth, "Can it be named…" began Rietta before meeting Carla's eyes. They smiled and said in unison, "'Scrufty'?"

The dog looked up at the sound of his new name being used. He looked from face to face for a moment before letting his fuzzy chin drop back to rest on his forepaws.

"So, with the tender loving care of the two sisters," Nanna continued, "Scrufty soon got stronger and, in no time at all, was running about their farm, chasing the chickens and wanting the girls to throw sticks. Soon, all its scars had healed and nice white fur grew so that the only pink left to see was the inside of its big, proud ears. One of its favourite things to do, though, was to roll in the mucky cattle yard until it was not white anymore, but an icky stinky brown!"

"Eeww!" chorused both girls with glee.

Nanna nodded down at the real Scrufty where he lay listening, "Don't go getting any ideas now."

"Actually, it was not too bad, though," she continued, "the girls just had to walk Scrufty down to the river and keep throwing a stick to get him to go in and out of the water over and over again, until the river washed him all clean and white again.

"Then, one morning the girls woke up to the sound of Scrufty barking outside and so they were up and out before they finished yawning to see what it was. What they saw was a group of three people standing outside their house.

"They were all strangers, and they could tell straight away that there was something special about them. There was a man and two young women. They were all very long and tall and thin and dressed in shiny fine clothes, and even though the only way to reach the farmstead was down the muddy track, their boots were gleaming like new and there was not a speck of mud anywhere on their fancy clothes.

"And… Scrufty was not barking at them to scare them away, he was wagging his tail and leaping with joy. He obviously knew these strangers and was very happy to see them. The man, who was the tallest of the three, and very handsome, bent down to make a fuss of the dog and Scrufty slobbered on his hands and even managed to lick his smiling face.

"Because Scrufty acted like that, the girls weren't afraid of the strangers, though they realised that they should have been – because it did not take them long to realise that these were no ordinary people. They were so tall, to start with! The man's hair was a gleaming black that was so shiny that it looked blue because it mirrored the sky. One of the girls had hair that shone like polished silver and the other had hair of pure gold. And they all had these big eyes that were the greenest green you'd ever seen. The girls knew that the strangers were 'of the Fae'."

"Fairies!" Carla and Rietta chorused, both sitting forward, hanging on every word.

"And, not just any old fairies! The man stood up and introduced himself as a fairy prince and the women were, his sisters, both princesses…

He explained that they had been searching the realm of the folk – that's what they called us 'normal' people – looking for their best hunting dog who had got lost when it chased away one of the Cwn Annwn…"

"Who are the Crooner Noons?" Carla interrupted.

"The Cwn Annwn are a pack of hounds from the underworld and Scrufty had bravely chased one away and through our world and right back to the underworld, but had obviously got hurt in the fight and collapsed before making it back home to their fairy fort.

"Well the handsome fairy prince and his beautiful princess sisters were so pleased, that the girls had looked after their dog so well, that they thanked them and, being fairies offered to pay them back, not with money, but by granting them three wishes.

"The fairy prince said, 'Thank you for looking after my favourite dog. You have done so well to make him better. To show my gratitude, I must do something for you in return. Now, I can smell your animals so strongly… I ask you, would like to have a cattle yard that never got soiled and never have to muck out the pigs ever again, never need to clean out filthy chicken coops?'"

"Well, of course this sounded good to the girls, but they had heard enough fairy stories to know that the Fae were tricksters and always set riddles to catch out the greedy and the lazy. They whispered to each other for a moment and then they politely said, 'No, thank you.'

"Was it because if they never had to clean out the animals again," Carla pondered, "it would mean they wouldn't have the animals anymore?"

"Yes, a clean cattle yard meant no cows – and that meant no milk, and never mucking out the pigs meant no more little piglets to sell at market, no more bacon for hard winters – and of course, no chickens, no eggs! Basically, it meant no more farm and quite probably starvation for the sisters and their family."

"So, the prince smiled an approving smile and said, "Well, then, perhaps my sisters can grant you a wish…"

Rietta suddenly sat forward in her chair and put the empty lemonade glass she had been cradling back onto the tray, "Oh," she whispered excitedly to Carla, "This wish bit's new!"

Nanna continued, "The two princesses stepped forward and bowed to the girls and the first, with hair of shining silver, said, 'I can grant you the wish you would make today…' and the second princess, with hair of gleaming gold, said, "Or, I can grant you the wish you would make tomorrow."

"Well the girls had to think hard about that – which wish would it be... Today's wish or tomorrow's?"

"Well," Carla pondered, "They say tomorrow never comes..."

"But," Rietta thought on, "They don't know what tomorrow will bring and perhaps they would really need that wish for something really serious..."

Carla nodded, "Like if one of them gets ill and needs to be made better... or something like that."

"I bet," Rietta said, "That they wanted to wish that Scrufty would stay with them..."

"But they can see how happy he is with his real owner..." Carla reasoned.

Rietta, who knew that too, pointed out, "They mustn't wish for anything that would be lazy or greedy to wish for..."

"No," Carla was emphatic, "'cos, then the fairies would turn it round into something bad by interpreting it in some clever-clogs kinda way…"

Nanna was nodding slowly with a gentle smile on her lips as she followed the girls reasoning, "So?" she asked, "Which wish would you two choose?"

The girls nodded in agreement and Rietta said, "Wish tomorrow."

"OK, then," Nanna picked up the story again, "So with that, the three fairies said farewell and walked away. The dog followed them with a wagging tail and although the girls were glad he had recovered and been reunited with his master, they felt very sad to see him go, especially as he did not hesitate or look back…"

"As the fairies reached the road, the sun rose above the crest of the mountains and its golden light fell upon them and it seemed to shine right through them. At that moment, the dog turned around and barked his farewell. By the time the barks echoed back from the mountains, the dog and the three strangers had already faded away into the dawn…"

Nanna Ivy left a pause, eyeing the two girls and seeing that they obviously hoped there was more to come. Birdsong and muffled music drifted in through the kitchen from the open back door. She continued.

"For the rest of the day, the girls did not say much – they were sad that Scrufty had to go, but they were also glad that they managed to make him better and that he was back with his master. They were also grateful to be cleaning out the animals – or rather they were grateful to have the animals to clean out, anyway."

"The next day, the girls got up and made themselves busy about their chores, trying not to feel sad even though they missed Scrufty a lot, and even with the cows mooing, the pigs squealing and snorting, and the chickens clucking around them, the little farm seemed quiet and a bit emptier, without the dog. But later that afternoon, they saw two people coming down the road – they recognised these two straight away –"

"Their Mum and Dad!" guessed Rietta.

Her Nan nodded, "And their parents had quite a tale to tell too!"

Rietta and Carla were both leaning forward, now, literally on the edge of the seats…

"It seems that their parents had done well in town. They had got there in time to catch the drovers and got a very good price for their geese from a rich merchant who paid them in gold coins.

"They had been hurrying back, walking all day every day and making use of the daylight until it got too dark to see. But they had the feeling that someone was following them… and last night, bandits had caught up with them. They must have seen them get paid in gold and followed them, until they were far enough away from town to waylay them and steal it.

"Now, their parents were brave and their father was a big strong man, but they were both unarmed and there were four bandits, two behind them with axes and two in front with knives. They knew from the look on the bandits' faces that they were not going to ask nicely for the gold and leave. Because the bandits had not bothered to cover their faces, they knew the bandits were not worried about ever being recognised again, which meant they intended to kill them both. But just then something strange happened.

"Suddenly, three strangers had appeared – they must have come out from among a nearby thicket – they were incredibly tall and dressed in fine clothes, and had a beautiful white hunting hound with them. Now, these people were obviously very wealthy. With greedy eyes, the bandits turned their attention to the three strangers – they were definitely worth robbing! But as the bandits turned, they changed…

"It was very dark by then, so it must have been a trick of the light, but as the four bandits raised their knives and axes to attack, they seemed to stretch and shrink all at once. Their legs grew crooked. Their heads stretched and their ears grew ridiculously long. They dropped their weapons as their hands became brown furred paws. And as their ears and limbs grew longer they also grew smaller, so that their clothes fell away from them… and, instead of four bandits, there were four rabbits on the road.

They sat hunched in their piles of clothes, with twitching noses and frightened eyes. Because right there in front of them was a huge, hungry looking, hunting hound.

"The rabbits turned tail and bolted off as fast as they could, with the big white dog chasing them into the darkness. Well, the girls' parents were stunned, as you can imagine, but they realised that even if it were just a trick of the light, those three beautiful strangers and their dog had just saved their lives. But when they searched the darkness to thank them, there was no sign of them at all. Just a faint echo as, somewhere in the distance, a dog barked…"

"So, that was the wish they would have made!" exclaimed Rietta, "– to have their parents back!"

Carla placed her empty glass back onto the tray, next to Rietta's, and then slid off her chair to sit on the rug close to Scrufty, she gently stroked the top of his head and asked, a little sadly, "Did they ever see Scrufty again?"

"It's not quite the end yet… is it Nanna?" said Rietta, knowingly.

"No – not quite: It turned out that, from then on, their cows gave the creamiest milk, and so their butter and cheeses became famous across the land, until word eventually reached the palace and the king put in a standing order for their famous cheeses. Their chickens laid the biggest, tastiest eggs every morning, without fail, even through the winter months – they always had enough to eat, and for baking, and plenty more for all their neighbours. And their pigs grew big and fat and had lots and lots of piglets. The farm prospered and the village became famous for its fine produce… and, no, they never saw the fairy dog again…"

Carla's brow ridged with sadness for a moment, until Nanna Ivy continued.

"But exactly one year later, to the day, since they had found the injured dog in that field, they were woken by a firm knock-knocking upon the farmhouse door. Their father opened the door but the girls could see that there was no one there. 'Come and look,' said their father, and the girls went to the door and saw, there on their step a little wicker-work basket lined with soft straw… and in the basket, was a tiny puppy, with big puppy-dog eyes – and pure white fur and pink ears… and when it looked at them both, it wagged its little tail… as if it already knew them…"

Carla's face had lit up, though her own big dark eyes still seemed a little teary, "That was a wonderful story," she said, "Thank you for taking the time to tell us!"

Chapter Ten

A Frightful Night

A storm front must have come over the valley in the night for Rietta was woken from a dream of dragons by the sound of rhythmic gusts buffeting the roof… but she could see stars through the window and gently swaying branches of trees delineated with moon-gleam as the sound faded. A few clouds drifted sleepily across the starry sky, but no sign of storm. Had she dreamt it entirely? The wind had sounded exactly like the beating of huge wings over the house. She stumbled to the window. One ankle tangled in her top-sheet and dragged it from the bed. There, outlined against a silvery halo of cloud, she thought she glimpsed the silhouette of a great winged beast, but could not be sure. It had faded before her eyes fully focussed and seemed to disappear through the cloud. Probably just the tail end of a dream.

She kept watching the sky for a little longer, revelling in the majesty of the moon as it paled behind shrouds of clouds and then slowly shed them again. When the moon dimmed, she could trace the trail of our own galaxy weaving its milky way between wispy clouds. She thought that, perhaps, her dream of magic wings would continue when she returned to sleep. So, she gathered up the fallen sheets and slipped back between them.

Although her eyes closed readily and she could almost glimpse dream pictures forming behind her eyelids, something was keeping her just awake. Another sound, an occasional quiet creak and soft thudding to a slow and random rhythm. She drifted closer to the dream pictures, a dragon smiled in the darkness, a dog ran along a shimmering path of scattered stars. Creak. Bump... bump... Sounded like the back door gently opening and closing with the breeze. A creature with a face of grey granite looked up at her window from the garden. The back door must have blown open in those stormy gusts...

She sat up suddenly, fully awake. The back door? Open? Scrufty?

She pushed the sheets back and rolled out of bed again, her feet finding their slippers as she switched on the toadstool bedside lamp. She plucked up her fleece from the floor and awkwardly navigated her uncoordinated arms into twisted sleeves as down the stairs she went. The soft thud sounded closer as she approached the kitchen doorway, which stood ajar, and beyond, she could see the moonlit garden path laying across the lawn like a ribbon of grey. The back door was open!

She immediately rushed into the living room to check that Scrufty was still in his bed. He was not.

She rushed out through the slowly swinging back door and into the garden, thinking he must have slipped out to check the perimeters. She peered around the patchwork of dark shapes, drifting in moonlight and shadow. "Scrufty!" she called, expecting him to appear, instantly, from behind a shrub or from around the side of the house. The garden seemed strange and otherworldly in this low light, set in motion by gentle gusts that tossed her uncombed hair. She lifted the pale strands from across her moon-blue eyes and looked down the path before her. The ironwork gate stood open to the fields beyond. Scrufty had gone.

She ran to the garden gate and called out into the darkness, "Scrufty!" This time louder. A squat shape moved away along the grassy path towards the woods. It was difficult to tell for sure if it had been the dog, because at that moment the moon was veiled by another band of cloud and the darkness swallowed all detail.

Zipping her fleece against the chilling breeze she followed, calling loudly one more time and looking back over her shoulder in the hope that her calls had woken up her parents. The faint glow from her nightlight lit the middle upstairs window from within, but the others remained dark, shining like black mirrors beneath the slate slope of roof.

Over the breath of the breeze, she was sure she heard another breathing, like the panting of an animal… and the grass-muffled footfalls of something trotting away ahead. Rietta picked up the pace, stumbling over unseen tumps.

If it was Scrufty she had seen and heard, he was obviously on the trail of something – maybe a badger on its nightly sojourn. Perhaps he was chasing a polecat back the woodland where it belonged. Or maybe just a neighbourhood moggy.

She was nearing the boundary fence to the woods and could not follow any further without going back for the torch. Standing there in the open night, she was aware of the valley around her, the loom of dark mountain slopes rising to cup the starry sky between their uneven peaks. She could hear the nearby brook plinking along, and an owl hoot-hooting in reply to another. The woods where Scrufty had been found lay before her like a dark, ground-bound cloud, its leaves whispering their secrets to the wind.

In desperation, she tried calling out again and again. She did not want to give up the chase if she was just moments behind Scrufty. She was straining her eyes to see through the shifting shadows between trees when moonlight flooded the vale once more, bright and shadow-casting after the deeper darkness in the shade of the clouds. Trees seemed to appear out of the formless dark before her eyes in a crazed pattern of silvered foliage and zigzag branches. Even with the moonlight, she could not be sure, but thought she saw a face in the shadows just a few paces into the woods. It was a broad face with a wide, lopsided mouth half hidden in the depths of a ragged hood. She felt the cold tingles run down her spine again and was momentarily transfixed with horror as the squat thing that was not quite human raised an arm and extended an angular finger towards her. Maybe she was still half asleep, maybe it was a creaking branch, but she thought she heard it say, "Come with me…" a dry rasping whisper floating on the breeze. In the vast darkness of night, without Carla by her side, she did not feel as brave as before. She turned and stumble-ran straight back the way she came, back up the garden path and into the dark house. She quickly closed the back door behind her and fumbled the bolt into place. She leant back against it, breathing hard for a moment, then hit the light switch. Her vision was bleary in the brightness and her cheeks were hot with tears.

After getting her breath back she charged up the stairs and to her parents' room, "Mum! Dad! Scrufty…" she choked back a sob, "Scrufty… he's gone! The door was open. Scrufty's gone…"

Henry had hurriedly dressed, putting his pants on over his pyjamas, and had gone out into the night to walk a wide circuit. For the half-hour or so he was gone, Sally sat with Rietta in the kitchen, and they sipped hot-chocolate.

"Scrufty'll be fine," Sally tried to reassure her daughter, "He's probably gone for an explore…

probably find his own way back in the morning."

"Do you think he might have gone off looking for his old home – his real owners?"

"Well, yes, perhaps he is homesick and now he's all better he wants to go back."

"But they abandoned him!"

"We don't know that, now do we?"

"Why was the door open?" Rietta's feelings of helplessness lent her voice an accusatory tone, "Who left it open?"

Sally was genuinely concerned about this, sure she had checked the door was locked, like she did last thing every night… "Maybe a burglar? And Scrufty chased him away."

"The police – we must phone the police!"

"If he's not back in the morning, then we shall."

They heard the front door open and close. Henry came into the kitchen, still shrugging off his coat and shaking his head.

Chapter Eleven

Wanted

When Rietta got up in the morning, Scrufty was not sat at the back door waiting. It was mid-morning when Carla called round. She could not believe Scrufty had gone, convinced that they loved him too much, and he loved them the same. He would never have just left them! So, mainly because it made them feel less helpless, the girls went out searching for Scrufty.

They decided to walk everywhere they could remember going with the dog, just in case he had gone for a big walk without them. They started at the great oak and walked the woodland path to the patch of bramble where they had found him. Rietta remembered flashes of what she had seen the night before, as they walked she recounted her experience to Carla. How she had run out into the night after Scrufty, and then seen the strange dwarf in the moonlit woodland, how it had pointed at her and whispered to her, asking her to follow. Carla was surprised Rietta had run away.

"You've seen that face, haven't you! No way was I going into the woods on my own – at night – to say, 'Hi,' to that creepy thing!"

"But it wanted to talk to you – it may still be the guide we need…" Carla paused to frown.

"What?" asked Rietta with concern, "What is it?"

"You don't think that thing wanted to talk to you so much it tried to come into your house?"

"You mean – it opened the back door?"

"And you know how Scrufty reacted, when he saw it before."

Rietta felt a little sick at the thought, "That dwarf-tramp-child-thing tried to break into my house? In the middle of the night? And Scrufty chased it off?" her face had paled, "You don't think it did anything to Scrufty, do you?"

Carla shrugged, "Bren and Maral wouldn't send something dangerous as our guide, would they?"

"Well, if it is the guide, why does it always run away?"

"Last night," Carla pointed out, "it was you who ran away, wasn't it?"

Rietta cocked her head, conceding the point, then asked, "Have you had any more fairy dreams?"

"Uh-huh," Carla nodded, "But not like before – I've just dreamt of the village as if I was seeing it on telly, or through the eyes of someone else living there. Like I used to. Nothing important happened, no more clues. I think they've been…" she shrugged, "just dreams… How'bout you?"

"Same here – I've had dreams with fairies in them, but that's nothing new. I think Bren and Maral were in one or two, but after I've been awake a few minutes, I can't remember them clearly… just dreams."

They walked over the bridge, through the neat little park, past the library, across the churchyard, past the shops. They called into ask Rietta's Nan if she had seen Scrufty. She had not. As it was nearly lunch time she offered the girls, "Sandwiches, or something on toast?" Rietta used her Nan's telephone to let her mother know where she and Carla were and to check if Scrufty had turned up at home.

He had not.

* * *

As they ate beans on cheese on toast, Nan suggested that they put a missing dog notice up at the library, and perhaps make some flyers for local shop windows, too. So, after a hurried lunch they thanked Nanna Ivy and went back to Rietta's to make posters.

Frustratingly, all the photos they could find of Scrufty, mainly on Sally's mobile phone, were so blurred it was not even clear they were of a dog, more like a brown, fuzzy cloud. Luckily, Rietta had sketched him several times and there was one particularly good drawing, in the dog-log, that she had spent time on getting right. So, they decided to use that. Carla thought the result looked like a wild-west 'Wanted' poster for an outlaw hound. Sad as they were, both girls managed a brief smile at what their efforts had produced.

They took their poster to the library where the head librarian greeted them both by name. This time she was wearing yellow drop earrings to match an ostentatious pair of spectacles. When the girls explained about Scrufty, she was very sympathetic and helpfully showed them how to use the photocopier to enlarge their design to a big poster, for the library and community centre notice board, and then reduced it to run off smaller copies as flyers. She did not even charge them for the copies.

They remembered how they had taken Scrufty to the library and looped his lead around the bicycle stand outside. He had not tried to make friends with other visitors as they came and went. He had not sulked or whined. He had simply sat there, with one ear up and one ear down, staring through the big windows, watching every move the girls made. He was a good dog.

* * *

By the time they had done the rounds of little shops, the supermarket, Post Office, and clinic, they had managed to get all the missing dog flyers pinned up on public notice boards or taped up in windows. Making the posters had helped to keep the girls from worrying. Doing something pro-active made them feel a little less helpless, but Rietta noticed how quiet Carla was as they walked up the street towards her aunty's maisonette.

"You OK?" asked Rietta.

Carla sort of nodded and shook her head at the same time. She slowed her pace and said, "I'm going to miss Scrufty so much…" She sniffed, obviously holding back the tears.

"Me too," agreed Rietta, "But let's not give up on him just yet, eh?"

"If it hadn't been for Scrufty, we might not have become such good friends so quick, don'tcha think?"

Rietta reached out and took hold of her friend's hands, "Y'want to know what I think?"

Carla nodded very seriously.

"I think we were already friends, before we even met…"

Carla gave a brief smile and her eyes sparkled as she said, "I used to spend many-a-day just waiting in anticipation of my dreams… they seemed like another life. I did not realise how lonely I had become when I had no one to share my dreams with… Now, with you, my days have been good too."

"Didn't you have friends before you came here?"

"Oh, yes. I had some good friends, ones I grew up with…"

"Well, then?"

"But as we got older, they were more into boy-bands and socks, and I started to feel silly talking to them about – about my dreams and fairies, and things like that… so I stopped."

"Well, if that's silly, then I'm just as silly as you are!"

"No!" Carla made a pretend offended face, "I'm by far the silliest!"

"You're too grown-up to be silly – It's me! I'm the silly one!" They both giggled and then hugged each other. They walked on quietly for a short distance, until Rietta said with a smirk, "Really? Socks?"

Chapter Twelve

Deep in the Dark Woods

Rietta sat up in bed. Something had woken her, again. Had it been a dream, or did she hear something from outside. Was it a whine? Was Scrufty back, waiting in the garden? He had left in the night, perhaps he had returned in the night. She leapt out of bed and across the landing opposite her bedroom door. She was confronted by her own, wide-eyed and pale reflection in the window, seemingly hovering in thin air. Beyond, the valley looked ghostly and insubstantial in the hazy light of a half-moon.

The gate was standing open. Yes, the whine had been the squeal of its metal hinges… and what was that? Rietta gasped sharply with a jolt of shock.

If it had remained still, it would have looked just like an out of place boulder. That would have been strange enough, right in the middle of their path, but… it was moving.

The creature was solid and squat, cowled in thick cloth, like weathered tarpaulin, mottled with lichens and velvety mosses, dragging fronds of damp moss and fern. Most chillingly, this mobile boulder had eyes and a face. It paused and looked up, the eyes flashing with sickly silver as they caught the moonlight and fixed upon Rietta. It was the thing from the woods – the too-old, grey and distorted features, the twisted lump-lipped mouth which now moved to form words that Rietta could hear like a whisper inside her head. "Come to me. Let me take you to This world of the Fair…" As the words floated up to her with the soft night-breeze, the creature raised an arm and beckoned up to her, "Come walk with me." Then it slowly turned its back and began to plod away along towards the gate.

"No, don't go…" breathed Rietta unable to call out for fear of waking her parents. She was both terrified and tremendously excited. The thing had just, quite clearly, identified itself as the guide, but she could not go on her own, not without Carla.

When it reached the end of the garden path it paused at the gate to beckon once more. "Come now to the woods…" came the impossibly quiet whisper that she could somehow hear, "I will wait for you…"

She could not clearly make out what then happened, because her quickening breath had clouded the window pane. She wiped it clear with a hand to see that the thing had gone from the gate. Then she glimpsed a dark shape moving away at quite a pace. Somehow it had folded in on itself, becoming a rounded boulder, and was rolling away up the shallow incline towards the head of the valley… and the woods.

Convinced that she was dreaming, Rietta tried not to think too hard lest her thoughts pull her out of sleep. Without flicking on the lights, and with a strong and strange sense of déjà vu, she made her way down the stairs and through the kitchen. She turned the key in the lock and opened the back door onto the night. The cool air brushed stray strands of her fine hair across her face and chilled her sleep-warmed cheeks. She reached for the red plastic raincoat that still hung next to the door, put it on over her pink-parrot pyjamas and, this time, remembered to pocket the little torch that had been left handy since night-time garden visits with Scrufty.

She stepped out into a misty summer's night. The humidity of the warm day had condensed on the cool air. The low moon was a thumb-smudge of silver just above the mountain peaks. Only the brightest stars pierced through the grey heavens.

Pausing at the garden gate, which remained open, she was aware of how quiet the night was. No sounds drifted down from the town. No end-of-a-night-out shouting or rowdy singing. No murmur of traffic, nor muffled door-slams. Rooves were silhouetted by a soft glow from the street lamps, but every house was sleeping, curtains closed and lights out.

She could hear the gentle burble of running water. Ghostly fronds of mist were snaking up from the mountain stream to explore between the reed-tumps, some trying to reach into the branches of her special tree where it stood like a dark sentinel. Was it whispering a warning to her? Just the light breeze amongst its leaves? The piercing shriek of an owl drew her attention. There – she glimpsed something at the fringe of the woods. The small, squat figure seemed to have been waiting for her to see it, for now it waddled away into the thick darkness between the trees.

As she neared the perimeter fence of the woods, she pulled out the torch and switched it on. The battery needed charging, but after the darkness it was bright enough to find the step-stile. She carefully climbed up and over, taking care not to snag the thin plastic of her coat on the barbed wire fence to each side.

The trees were all softly whispering, repeating the warning that her special tree had tried to give her. There was also the sound of heavy feet crunching through leaf-litter and fallen twigs. The weak beam of torchlight showed her the path that lead into darker shadows beyond.

Her own footsteps drowned out the sounds of the creature she was following, so she repeatedly paused to listen and check if it still moved ahead of her. Then another, louder sound. It could have been startled birds in the tree tops, or a stray sheep panicking at her approach. A sudden rush of rustling motion, then quiet. She stood still and listened. Just the breeze in the leaves.

Then, that whisper inside her head again, "Help!" it called with an edge of desperation. She swung the torch beam from side to side, setting the tree-trunk shadows into a dance of darkness and light. Two pin-points flashed back at her from a thicket of pale, thin saplings. Eyes. She let out a gasp of shock. The torch beam rested on the stern stony face, now contorted into a leer of abject terror. It certainly had no sense of threat. "Heelllp… mmeee…" came the dread-laden whisper. Her first impulse was to run, but this was a plea for her help. Her own voice startled her when she called out, "What's wrong?" frantically scanning the torch back and forth. The woods were an abstract tangle of bright branches and dark hollows that all seemed to move with the swinging beam. Thick mist hanging in the tree-tops transformed the scant light into searchbeams. She could see nothing else in the woods surrounding them. Despite her building fear, she took a few tentative steps forward. If this was indeed a dream, she would surely be waking up any moment.

As she approached, she realised that the thicket of silvery hazel or birch saplings were the extenuated, bone-white fingers of some dark creature that had the squat thing in its grasp. Looking up she saw that the mist in the canopy was moving like thick smoke within a defined 'rib-cage' of branches and boughs. Hanging above her, barely discernible in the darkness was a huge and hideous hooded head. She shone the torch beam up at its face and instantly regretting doing so. Like its fingers of branches, the face was disturbingly elongated, the mouth a sharp, inverted chevron. She saw no other recognisable features except its eyes... so black that the torchlight was being swallowed into them like twin black holes, sucking in everything from light years around. Then the chin distended impossibly, revealing rows of moon-silver teeth in a shark-like sneer. It screamed at her.

The sound was more terrifying and strange than any scream could be, high pitched like a shrieking girl, but with an underlying hollow rushing like the roll of distant thunder, or a storm wind sucking at an ill-fitting door. It contained modulated textures, as if words of horrific profanity were about to take form. Words that could corrupt, debauch, injure and perhaps even kill. She had heard similar sounds from the throats of people in extreme grief, at funerals, or in harrowing war documentaries – but this was different, there was a definite tone of threat that outweighed any sense of despair.

Rietta was so scared that she too screamed – and ran toward the grotesque thing, arms flailing, not even realising that she had picked up a rock and was throwing it whilst shouting the worst swear words she had heard the older boys at school use to insult each other. Somehow, she realised that it would be pointless to run away from it.

The tall thing reared away from the other, squat thing and swirled upward until its pale, distended visage was crisscrossed with the whipping branches of willow. The bone-white claws stretched impossibly along the path toward Rietta and then suddenly dispersed, as if sucked away into the surrounding darkness, lost in a fold of the night. Then silence, disturbed only by the fluttering of something large and winged in the high branches, a sleeping buzzard or raven disturbed by the commotion…

The smaller creature remained crouched and cowering where it was. She was aware of a quiet sobbing, pathetic and wheezing. She gulped and started breathing again. Her heart was pounding as she approached the frightened thing.

Its face was almost twice as wide as it was long. Like some squashed caricature. The skin a muddish blue-black dark, deeply folded, cracked and scuffed like the leather of a well-worn satchel. Above a solid broad chin, the mouth was hideously wide, the lips unevenly twisted so it was hard to tell if it wore a sneer or a smile. Slab-like teeth glistened in the dark behind the lips like pale quartz stones. The knobbly upper lip merged with the broad flattened nose and strangely, the nostrils closed tight between in-breath and out-breath. The eyes were a glistening grey, like slate runestones laying in the bed of a stream, their only colour was caught in their pupils when they occasionally flashed luminous green in the torchlight, like the eyes of a wild thing caught in the beams of car headlamps at night. Those eyes met hers with an uncertain expression somewhere between fear and thankfulness.

Rietta just about managed to find her voice and asked, "What even are you?"

The creature's voice was a dry whisper as it said, "Thank you, for saving humble mokrok."

Rietta nervously swung the fading torch beam around the hollow they were in, "Will that thing come back?"

"You sent skilk away!"

"Wha-what's a... skilk?"

"Skilks are bad ones."

"…and mokrok? That's your name?"

"No name. Mokrok is what I am. Mokroks are good ones."

"You were sent by Bren and Maral?"

The thing did not seem to comprehend the simple question, "You woke me. Now I am to show you the way…"

The torch light almost dimmed to nothing. Rietta shook it, in an unsuccessful attempt to revive it. "Let's get out of the woods," she urged, "before the battery runs out completely."

She quickly retraced her path toward the edge of the woodland with the crunching footsteps of the mokrok following her. As they reached the perimeter fence, she heard a louder commotion from behind and turned around in alarm, half expecting to see the terrifying skilk swooping at her from the tree tops again. Instead, she saw that the odd, little mokrok had reverted into boulder form and was rolling down the bank toward the river. With a familiar sound of splashing, it then rolled along and out of sight though the gap under the fence. Rietta carefully climbed over the stile and saw the dark, squat form waiting for her a short distance along the path toward home.

Now she was away from the deep darkness of the woodland, the light of the moon was much brighter than her fading flashlight. She switched it off. The mokrok was at her side again saying, "Take me to the waystone now and we will pass through."

"You mean go now? To the fairy-world?"

The heavy head nodded, "The Fair Ones? They need you now. Need you to help them… can't let them down!"

"Well, they've waited this long, and I have a few questions first…"

The mokrok simply said, "Ask your questions. I may have answers."

"Well, what's your name for a start?"

"I told you, I have no name… Can't name – names come from you Hume Ones. You dream new words and the things they name come true. We need to take your words to make our names. Not all have names… Lonely, the nameless ones become. Some stay sad and formless. Bitter and hateful sometimes too, you see… Your name?"

She was shaking her head incredulously, "My name? Rietta."

"Oooh," the dull eyes widened as he looked up in awe, "– see, Hume Ones say it so easy – take it all for granted!"

"That's silly. How do you name new things?"

"New things need new words…" It was not an answer to her question, but before she could press him on the subject, he continued, "Some words are spell-words and names are powerful spells. The Hume Ones can wield spell-words so well – that is how you will help those who need you. Just like you used your words to send the skilk away and save me, just now…" He looked back towards the woods.

She thought about this. There was no other obvious reason why the super-scary skilk had reacted in such a way and fled from an unarmed young girl. All she had done was shout at it and throw a stone…

The mokrok's eyes flicked from side to side and he leant forward in a conspiratorial gesture, "You come through with me, to this world I speak of and you'd be mighty powerful. You would help many good against many bad. You see?"

"Not really, no…"

"Ah, yes – not too good with the words, me, you see – come and I'll take you to meet those who can explain it all to you." The hefty head nodded vigorously. "You trust me?"

"I can't." Rietta protested, although part of her wanted to, now that her fear had subsided and a sense of adventure returned, "I'm not supposed to be out at all. I've got to get back home!" Decisively, she started walking away.

The creature shuffled after her, "You can. After this world. You visit. You come back. You go home."

Well, put that way, it sounded very simple. "But I have to be back before I'm missed."

"We go there by a waystone, so you come back the same time you leave. If you come with me. Now. You will come back... Now."

"What?" Rietta paused, "I go to this fairy world of yours, and then I can come back, and no time will have passed in my world?"

He seemed to think about that for a moment, his eyes rolling as if making a calculation, "Minutes, maybe. But more-or-less no time. No-yes?" The mokrok reached up and gently tugged the plastic sleeve of Rietta's coat at the elbow, raising a stony eyebrow enticingly. "You come, eh?"

"OK, but not tonight… I have to tell a friend."

With that she started walking away, and the mokrok called after her, "…it better not take too long – or I'll call you some new names you might not like!"

She turned and saw that his wide mouth had stretched into a crazy grin.

She let out an exasperated sigh, "OK – so where will I be able to find you again?"

"No worry about that," it waddled up to her side, "I come with you now…"

"You can't. I'm going home."

"I need to be near you…" it said, walking close at her heels, "Protect me, you did do, from the skilk. Please be kind!"

The little rock man followed her the short distance back until she paused at the back gate to say, "Right, you could wait over by the tree, where you had been for centuries…"

"No…" its eyes peered pleadingly up at her, they seemed to have grown larger and shone in the moonlight as if teary, "If skilk takes me – I cannot take you. You never be able to help those people in this world I speak of…"

"Oh…" she thought about it for a moment then crouched down to be at the same eye level, "But you'll have to be very quiet."

"I can be as silent as a stone," the mokrok promised

As she opened the back door, Rietta felt a pang of sorrow. She half expected Scrufty to come running, barking at the top of his lungs at the little stone man that followed her into the kitchen. Her parents would have been there in moments to see what the kerfuffle was all about… Alas, there was no such greeting as she shrugged out of the red kagool and hung it on its peg.

It was very dark in the house. Everything was made up of dark shapes, some greyer that others, some blacker than those. It was a monochrome patchwork that she only partially recognised, but she was familiar enough with her surroundings to overcome her apprehensive ill ease and so make her way back upstairs. The stairs creaked under the weight of the mokrok and every board of the landing seemed to complain, or at least comment, about their progress past the door to her parents' room and towards hers. The door to Rietta's room stood ajar in the rectangle of moonlight that shone through the window.

Rietta gently closed the door behind them with nothing more than a soft click and took a deep breath of relief. The room was still lit by the toadstool lamp. The mokrok waddled around the foot of her bed towards the front window where he paused. "I thank you," he said in his dry, wheezing whisper, "I sleep here?"

Rietta nodded, "Suppose so…" she had not fully convinced herself that this course of action was quite the right thing. The thought crossed her mind that, perhaps, this was all part of a dream just like her visit to Dreamers Dell. Maybe the mokrok would no longer be there when she awoke in the morning.

The creature knelt down as if looking very closely at the floor, drew its knees to it midriff with a grinding sound against the floorboards. "I do not sleep the sleep of centuries this time," it whispered, "Just knock on my head to wake me, three times should do." With that it tucked its elbows in against the knobbly knees and bowed the ungainly head until it touched the floor. There was a strange sound that Rietta felt in the bones of her skull rather that heard with her ears and once more, the mokrok looked exactly like the mossy boulder from near her special tree.

Without taking her gaze from the rock, she sat onto the edge of her bed. She kicked off her slippers, which were cold and damp from the dewy grass outside. She laid back and reached out to turn off the bedside lamp, pulling the sheets up to her chin against the chill. She lay on her side and could not help but stare at the dark hunched shape of the stone. After a couple of minutes, she swung her legs from under the sheets and sat on the edge of the mattress. She tugged the extra, woolly tartan blanket from the foot of the bed and draped it over the boulder before lying back down and turning away onto her side.

Very quietly, a muffled voice nearby said, "Nighty-night."

She closed her eyes and hoped that sleep would soon come. It could not be long until morning. Perhaps she could dream herself back to the fairy village and get some answers from Maral and Bren. She could hardly wait for Carla to call round and meet the mokrok. Scrufty – She still hoped that he would find his own way home. Perhaps he would be waiting at the back door in the morning. Maybe the mokrok would be gone with her dreams, but the dog would be back…

She chased such thoughts around in her head. One moment she felt sad and worried about Scrufty. Then she was filled with excitement and elation at meeting a magical being who would guide them to the world of fairies. But now, she really needed to sleep, yet her mind was swirling with these thoughts, dilemmas and doubts. She saw images of dark woodland paths and terrible downturned mouths yawning with supernatural screams. She did not notice the point when her disordered thoughts became dark dreams.

Chapter Thirteen
Meet Lee

On her arrival, Carla had been very sad about Scrufty's failure to return. Henry, who was working from home for the day had made them some tea, "Nothing like a good panad o' builders tea to bolster the spirits…" he said. The teas were too hot to guzzle quickly and Henry was kindly trying to take their minds off the missing dog.

"I'm preparing for a meeting with the P-S-I…" He nodded to the maps and plans he had laid out on the dining table. He rolled one, large map out more fully, covering others. To hold it down he used the corner of his open laptop, the salt and pepper pots, and a brass dragon candle-holder for paper weights. The map showed an area with lots of crammed contour lines that indicated steep slopes, peaks and valleys. The mountainous terrain was scattered with clusters of colour-coded and numbered dots.

"What is the pea-essay?" asked Carla.

Henry smiled, "Plant and Seeds Institute. They look after natural habitats and collect seeds form endangered plants…"

Carla understood, "They're conservationists?"

"Exactly. Well, this map shows a plan for a big road that I'm helping to build. These red squares," he tapped the map, "show places where there are very old things, under the ground, mainly little bronze age villages and some Roman forts. So the road has to avoid those places… Now these coloured stickers," tap-tap, "have been kindly added to the map by the Plant and Seeds Institute, to show population densities of rare plants. Now, some of these plants are so very rare that they don't grow anywhere else in the whole world! So, if we dig them up to build the road…"

"They'd be extincted," Rietta said with an air of finality.

"Uh-huh," Henry nodded, "So, I have to redesign the route of the road to avoid disrupting those unique habitats." He paused, realising he could easily lapse into professional jargon. He tapped an area on the map where dots of every colour were densely clustered. "Here," he said, "There are two types of orchid that grow nowhere else, and… well they haven't counted the different kinds of fungi, yet! They discovered a new kind of toadstool there – looks just like one a caterpillar might sit on to smoke his pipe."

Carla seemed fascinated, though Henry sensed that Rietta was a little distracted. "And here," he tapped a cluster of black rectangles at one corner of the map, "is where we are… not too far… So, I was thinking – if you girls were up for it – perhaps this weekend, we could go and have a picnic there. You could do a little nature project, see if we can find those rare orchids and mushrooms?"

The girls agreed that would be a great idea. Carla pointed to one of the small black rectangles and asked, "Is that where we are right now?" Henry nodded, "That's our house, yes." Carla traced a straight line from the house, through where their special ancient oak would stand, across the tiny square-and-cross symbol indicating the church, and finally tapped an area in among the cluster of squares that was the main town, "There. That's where I live."

"Perhaps," Henry said, "We all live on a leyline…"

"Leyline?" Rietta queried over the rim of her tea mug.

"Some people think that important places are connected by invisible lines of mystical energy and all the lines meet in the middle of Stone Henge…"

Carla suggested that they look for other leylines, but Rietta said they had to leave her dad alone to concentrate on his work and suggested, perhaps a little too eagerly, that they should go up to her room to, "Do some drawing. Now."

"That's the big rock!" Carla's eyes flicked from her friend to the rock and back again. Rietta – rock – Rietta – rock. "Is it? The rock from by our tree?"

Rietta, leaning back against the closed door to her room simply nodded.

Carla asked the obvious question, "How did it get up here?"

Rietta grinned mischievously, "Why don't you ask it?"

Carla raised one of her dark eyebrows and Rietta wafted at her with both hands saying, "Go on, take a closer look!"

Carla moved around the foot of the bed and crouched down to inspect the boulder. It definitely was the same rock, she could recognise it from its basic shape and pattern of mosses. Suddenly she squealed and leapt back, "It – it…" she spluttered, "It looked at me!" She could not take her eyes from the rock as it began to transform in front of her. "It's got eyes, Rietta! It has eyes!" A lumpy-knuckled hand lifted away from the main mass and waved at her. "It has hands!" she gasped, "It's…"

The rock chuckled like an old leather satchel filled with gravel and then said, "Hello to you too, two-of-two!"

"Don't worry," Rietta reassured, "He's friendly…" She had moved around the bed to stand at her friend's side, "You are, aren't you?"

"I am. What?" the mokrok had now unfolded and stood upright before them.

"Friendly."

"Friend?" The wide mouth seemed to twist into something like a smile of surprise, "Yes, I am, but I did not know my name was – Lee!" His eyes rolled from side to side as he pondered, "I like 'Lee'! I'll take it. Thank you!"

"What…" Carla found her voice again, "What is he talking about?"

"Erm," Rietta sounded just as puzzled, "He thinks I just named him, Lee…" she sat onto the edge of the bed and said, "Carla, meet Lee, the mokrok!"

Carla extended an arm as if to offer a hand, thought better of it and awkwardly sat down next to Rietta. With the mokrok standing on its stubby legs, his eyes and theirs were level as they sat. Carla managed to look away from the creature for a moment to fire a questioning frown at Rietta who had already opened her sketch book on her lap and was attempting to draw the mokrok. She recounted the partly dream-like, partly nightmarish events of the previous night. Carla struggled to follow Rietta's jumbled sentences, in which words collided and tripped over one another. When Rietta reached the part about yelling at the skilk and how her words worked like a spell, the mokrok said,

"Yes, luckily, a Hume has such great power. You saved lucky Lee!"

The first thing Carla asked was, "So, you're our guide?"

The mokrok shrugged, "I am here to get you there. We must go while things are all in order. Waystone is easier to open this time of year. But getting harder, every day we wait."

"OK, so what is a waystone?" asked Rietta at the same time as Carla asked, "Where is this gate-way-stone?"

The mokrok studied their faces for a rather off-putting moment, then he said, "I thought you would know…" He sounded sad, defeated, "I have slept the sleep of centuries here, and when I dozed away, all that long time ago, waystone was at my side. They don't usually move, but I hear that happens more and more nowadays."

Rietta stopped sketching and asked, "Hear? Hear from who? You just said you'd been asleep for hundreds of years."

"When I sleep in one world, I walk awake in another." He raised his right hand and said, "Awake in one world," then raised his left hand, "Asleep in another." There was a touch of pride in his voice as he added, "We are the only ones who can do this."

Rietta tried to explain more to Carla, "So our rhyme woke him and made a connection to the fairy world, and that's how we could go there in a dream… well, we weren't just dreaming that time. The fairies were able to come and… take us there… but?" her voice slowed as she thought hard about how to explain something she did not fully understand and her explanation turned into a question instead, "So, only part of us could pass through, nothing material, just our spirit, our dream-selves?"

"Right! Yes, good." The mokrok sounded like a teacher who had been surprised by a pupil unexpectedly hitting on the correct answer to a difficult problem, "The only way for material bodies to pass through is by waystone."

"But…" Carla was still struggling to comprehend, "You're –"

"Already here," the mokrok cut-in, "Or there. Depending how you look at it. I am a part of the ancient lands, from times before the partitioning."

"Fine," Rietta picked up on this reasoning, "So what about that skilk thing?"

"Skilks are wraiths. Have no material body. The partitions are thin enough in places for them to be pushed through," his pebble-grey eyes rolled as if searching for a better explanation, "– like the dreams. But skilk can use material they find to make bodies – anything that is now dead but once lived, they can use."

Rietta nodded, "Deadwood in this case."

Carla continued the interrogation, "So who, or what, pushed the skilk-wraith through?"

The mokrok made a 'who knows?' gesture with both hands, "Maybe mumblebones. Maybe…" and his voice dropped to a whisper, as if afraid to say, "the Other Ones…" then, louder again, "Someone who wants to stop me helping you. Almost had me too. But no match for you, young Hume one!" His leathery lips twisted into what Rietta took to be a grateful smile, "You have more power than you know."

"So, why us?" Rietta still was not convinced they were the right girls for the job.

The mokrok repeated his cryptic phrase, "Because you have more power than you know…" He sensed the girls' frustration and continued, "Because, a long spell is running deep. Spells are patterns. Patterns of words, patterns of happenings. Patterns of deeds done and yet to be done. You are both part of the pattern. You used a pattern to connect this world to that world? A pattern that woke me?"

It took a moment to realise that he had asked a question, "Oh," Rietta flicked through a few pages of her sketch pad and showed him a double spread filled with different designs based on the pattern they had laid-out with twigs, formed by their combined initials, "You mean this?"

His eyes narrowed as he scanned the page and asked, "It has meaning to you?" His brow rose dubiously.

"Our initials…"

Carla explained further, "We put together the first letters of our names…"

"Ah-ha!" the mokrok nodded, "Names, you see. Powerful spell-words – powerful pattern… Now, I am also part of your pattern. All parts of the pattern coming together… but an important part is missing."

"What's missing?" Carla asked.

The mokrok held a hand up before his broad face and counted out on his fingers as he spoke, "Carla, Rietta, Lee – that would be me!" He waggled the fourth finger and said, "Waystone." He then gestured with open hand as if passing the explaining over to the girls.

"We don't know anything about waystones!" they protested together.

"Very big waystone," the mokrok sounded exasperated, "Can't miss it!"

They shook their heads. "Might be in a museum," suggested Carla, and Rietta followed on with, "Or built into someone's house…

maybe even the old bridge – there are some huge stones in that."

"We must locate waystone." Lee, the mokrok was emphatic, "Or you will fail those relying on you."

"Relying on us for what, though?" Rietta huffed.

"Yes. That is what we would like to know," reiterated Carla a little more calmly.

"Save them. Repel mumblebones and," in a whisper again, "the Other Ones…" He looked dramatically from one to the other. "You can save This Realm of the Fair Ones and That Realm of the Hume Ones…" His face started to cloud over in puzzlement again, "Oh, so confusing for my little brain of flint! You see, to me this is that world, and that is this world! But, whatever way you look at it, both our worlds need to be protected from… from those of …another realm."

Carla nodded as if she understood, but Rietta asked, "But how can we do that?"

"If I knew," the mokrok tilted his head to look at her askew, "It would be me not you they need, huh?"

"But we're just…" Rietta shrugged, "Us. What could we possibly do to help the Fair Ones?"

"You saw what you can do!" Lee, the mokrok nodded, "Last night – the skilk, One of the darkly powerful ones and you sent it away with just a few magic words!"

"They weren't exactly 'magic' words," Rietta leant a bit closer to Carla and added, "I just swore at it…"

"The words you say become spells…" His brows jostled and his nostrils opened and closed with a few breaths as he considered how to better explain, "It is your spell-words that can protect this and that world from all the darkly powerful ones who want so much to rule again… Surely you must already know this from your long word patterns – your oldest stories – they tell of these things."

"You mean like heaven and hell?" Rietta asked.

"Or," Carla said, "The Viking, legends of Midgard, Asgard… Valhalla…"

"Olympus and Hades…" added Rietta.

Lee the mokrok was nodding, seemingly satisfied that they, at least partly, understood. He said, "Waystone is our gateway between."

Carla suggested, "Perhaps we could find something at the library, don'tcha think?"

"And we can ask Nanna Ivy," now Rietta was warming to the whole idea, "She knows local history."

"Yes-yes!" said the mokrok and waddled towards the bedroom door, "Let us go and find the waystone at the library."

"No-no!" cried Rietta tossing aside her pad and tumbling across the bed to stand and block his exit, "You can't come!"

His stony face took on a hurt expression so Rietta explained, "Look, you spent all this time being all mysterious and careful that only we saw you. You can't just go walking about in broad daylight for all to see. I mean, what would they do with you?"

"Ah, yes…" he conceded, "Your point is good. But if waystone is at this library, then we must –"

"It is not going to be at the library. Books are at the library. History books that just might mention the stone and what happened to it…"

Chapter Fourteen
Referencing the Stone

They arrived at the library just as clouds had rolled across the sky and the first few big raindrops were darkly dotting the pavement. At the back of the library, between two 'sleeping' computer workstations, there was an oversized, heavy door of age-darkened wood. Above it was a semi-circular, stained-glass fanlight with the words 'Public Library' worked into the leaded design. A brass plaque fixed to the door itself had the word 'Reference' engraved across it in the best Victorian cursive lettering. Rietta had noticed in passing on previous visits, but always dismissed it as a disused back door.

"You see," explained the librarian, "When the library was modernised, they built the new part as an extension to the old building…" This time her neon-blue earrings and spectacle frames added a dramatic splash of colour to her black blouse and beige corduroy skirt. "This used to be the front door…" She pushed open the door and showed them through to a section of the library that Rietta had not known to exist.

The reference section was darker than the main library and smelt of old leather and wood polish. The floor was a gleaming wood-block pattern and bookshelves stood, floor-to-ceiling between fluted wooden pillars. The ceiling was high, patterned with an embossed lattice of plaster work, and half-way up a gallery with iron railings ran along all four walls allowing access to the higher shelves. At the far end, the gallery broadened into a mezzanine reached via a spiral staircase. Above that was a row of four, stone-framed casement windows, each with different stained-glass coats of arms. It was like stepping from the present-day of the new library and into the past.

Most of the books were big and leather-bound. Some were in multi-volume sets that filled several feet of shelving. Others were in special bookcases, locked behind metal grilles.

The librarian led them up the spiral of iron stairs and along the gallery. "Local history," she announced grandly. She produced a bunch of keys from her skirt pocket and selected an old one of black metal to open one of the shutters that protected the older books. "Now, let's see…" she pondered, "Why don't we start with this one?" She hefted a huge book from the shelf and carried to the reading area that occupied the mezzanine.

"Is that a book, or a suitcase?" said Carla, in awe of the size of the antique volume.

A long reading table ran along the mezzanine, the green glass shades of its desk lamps gleaming in the light from the casement windows above it.

"You'll find plenty in here," said the librarian, tapping the gold inlaid cover of scuffed brown leather. She then unfastened a hasp and unclasped the big book.

"Books," she said, looking down at the two girls who were obviously eager to get into the pages, "Books can be many things… Sometimes books are people – their thoughts, ideas, memories, captured and preserved between two covers. There can be whole worlds within a book… and some books are time machines, like opening a door to the past and, sometimes, even the future." She nodded thoughtfully and said,

"I'll leave you girls to explore the contents of this one."

From halfway down the spiral staircase she called, "Let me know if you need any more help." Then her footsteps tapped across the woodblocks below and the big door squealed closed behind her.

The book creaked as the girls carefully opened it together, releasing a smell of must and dust. The clasp had been there to stop several unbound sections from falling out and being lost. There were ledgers, long lists of names and dates, detailed maps, and plans that unfolded to cover the large tabletop. Some of the pages were of a rougher, yellowed paper, crammed with columns of small print. Others were easier to read with larger print on a paper of better quality. The girls noticed some pages that looked like tracing paper and when they opened the book at these, they found them to be entirely blank. The purpose of those leafs was solely to protect the pages immediately following, which were full-page illustrations, including some fine engravings on thick shiny paper and a few hand-tinted photographs.

There was a pattering of rain against the windows, and perhaps a distant rumble of summer lightning. Otherwise, it was quiet in the library. Handling the antique book had instilled a sense of reverence. Rietta and Carla had the entire reference section to themselves, yet they still conversed in whispers as they diligently set about their research. They were too engrossed to notice exactly when the rain had ceased. They noticed that the windows had brightened, making the small print easier to read and that sunshine was projecting patterns of heraldic colours across the table from the stained-glass coats of arms.

The book was a detailed history of their village and the surrounding locale, charting its growth over centuries: Neolithic hut circles, bronze-age mines in the mountainsides, iron-age artefacts in the marshlands, a bangor-fenced enclosure surrounding a simple wooden hut next to a great standing stone…

Sally did not explain why she wanted Henry to follow her up to Rietta's room, she simply asked him to accompany her and when they entered she gestured to the room in general. Henry looked the room over. There were some books on the floor along with a scattering of cuddly toys. A drawing pad and a handful of pencils had been tossed onto the rumpled duvet of the bed. Beneath the window, on the far side of the room by the wardrobe, there was what appeared to be a pile of clothes with a blanket tossed over it.

"Needs a bit of a tidy?" he guessed.

Sally nodded to the tartan blanket that covered the something in the far corner, "Have a look under there – I kicked my toe on it when I came in to open the window."

The expression on Henry's face changed from bafflement to concern as he made his way around the foot of the bed, bent down and pulled back the blanket to reveal…

"It's a rock!" he said, surprised and with a hint of relief that it had not been anything worse. He bent down to look more closely at it, running a hand across the dry moss-covered top. He glanced back at the bed and reached for Rietta's drawing pad which was laying open on a double page. There were rough sketches of the rock from different angles. She had even added some brief annotations of details: the 'veins of quartz', the 'patterns of lichen' that resemble 'maps of unknown lands?' In the biggest, most careful of the drawings, Rietta had added faces and hands, turning the rock into some sort of goblin creature.

Henry held the pages open towards Sally, "Not bad, eh? She's been using it for artist's reference…"

Sally nodded, still looking uneasy, "OK," she said, "But it should not really be in the house, should it… do you think you could put it back outside?"

"Alright…" Henry put the pad back on the bed and bent to lift the boulder. On his first attempt, it would not budge. He adjusted his posture, back straight, using his leg muscles to do the lifting. He grunted with the effort and the rock moved an inch or so, grinding into the floorboards. He looked back over his shoulder at Sally, still standing in the doorway.

"Rietta couldn't've…" he began.

Shaking her head, Sally finished his sentence, "…not even with Carla's help."

"So how the heck did it get up here?" Henry frowned, and in a voice tinged with worry said, "You think someone else helped them?"

"Well it didn't walk all the way up here by itself."

She finally came into the room and sat on the edge of the bed. Henry stood up and joined her, staring at the sunny day outside the window, he said quietly, "Have you asked Rietta about it?"

"They went to the library," explained Sally, "and they're calling in to my mum's… to hear some of her Nanna's tales of the valley in the olden days. Still hoping to find the dog, on the way." She sighed, "They'll both be back for tea."

"You think it may be Carla's influence…"

Sally shrugged, "She seems such a nice girl, and they're the best of friends already, but we don't know much about her background, do we?"

"I'll slice some more?" said Rietta's Nan, picking up the flower pattern plate dusted with cake crumbs and frosting.

"Thank you," Rietta said, quickly adding, "but we'll be having tea as soon as we get back."

"How about you, Carla?"

"I'm going round for tea, too. It was lovely cake," she patted her own belly, "but I have to leave some room."

Nanna Ivy had already bustled out to the back kitchen when she called back, "You'll finish off the lemonade, though." It was more a command than an offer.

"Yes, please." chorused the girls. Rietta's Nanna made fresh pressed, still lemonade with just enough sugar to mask the sharpness without affecting the zing. Perfect for washing down creamy, crumbly carrot cake.

There was some clattering and clinking from beyond the door as Nanna continued talking, "So, the history of the valley? What was it you were wanting to find out?"

"Someone told us that there was once a big standing stone next to the Great Oak…" said Rietta, "We were just trying to find out about it in the library…"

"And what did you find out?" Nanna returned from the kitchen, carefully carrying a wooden tray laden with a large glass jug of cloudy lemonade, prettily decorated with golden silhouettes of flowers around the base and birds in flight at the rim to match the two tall tumblers. She placed the tray on the crocheted circle that centred the top of a gleamingly polished dark wood table.

"The Librarian found us a big book," Rietta continued, "about the history of the county and there was an old drawing –"

"A 'highly accomplished woodcut of exceptional quality' by an unknown artist from the Medieval period," Carla quoted.

"It was very nice," smiled Rietta, "And it showed the valley when the first church was built. A wooden one…"

"Oh, yes…" said her Nanna to let them know that she was listening whilst concentrating on filling both glasses brim-full.

"…And in the background, you could see our oak tree and right there, next to it, was this huge stone."

"Almost as tall as the tree!" Carla commented.

"The tree must have been smaller back then, though," reasoned Nanna with a raised eyebrow, passing each girl a lemonade.

"Thank you," they said, each taking their glasses in both hands to steadily raise them to their lips without spillage. They could not help but drink down several gulps at once, it was so refreshing.

"Yes," agreed Rietta, "But what happened to it? Where did it go?"

"Well," her Nanna sat back in her comfy armchair, "Wood doesn't last long in our damp environment. Grows well when it is still a living tree, of course. But exposed timber rots and gets woodworm, so they rebuilt the church with stone, in the early sixteen-hundreds, I think, perhaps before… A few bits were added over the centuries, until it became the village church we know today."

"The standing stone, though," clarified Carla, "What happened to the big standing stone – it's not next to the tree anymore."

"I was coming to that…" Nanna smiled, "That standing stone was a marker for the pre-historic people who first settled in the valley. It was a crossing point, where they could safely cross the boggy marshlands back then. Some say, it was a spiritual marker too, a place where the world of men and the world of the gods met…"

Carla and Rietta exchanged knowing glances as Nanna Ivy continued, "They had worshipped there for hundreds and thousands of years, until they eventually heard about Christianity, gave up their pagan magic and converted – that would have been just after the Romans gave up squabbling with the Celts and took themselves back off to Rome…" She paused briefly and glanced at the bright window, its light glinting on her spectacles, "The wooden church was a sort of stop-gap until the monks drummed-up plenty of followers who could help build a bigger, better one." She looked back to the girls who listened intently, both peering over their glasses of lemonade, "So when they built the stone church, they wanted a grand, significant and symbolic stone altar…"

She paused to enjoy the looks of realisation sweep across the bright young faces before her.

"The standing stone!" Rietta blurted out, and Carla re-iterated, "They used the standing stone for the altar… is it still there?"

"It was a huge stone, god knows how they moved it at all – no cranes, no tractors, just horses and logs, and pulleys – some say that it was god who showed the monks how to do it, in a vision, others say that it walked there all by itself, propelled by the power of prayer… but it was so big that they placed it there first and then built the church around it. So yes, it is still there and will have to stay there, as long as the church still stands."

The girls exchanged excited looks, Carla asked Rietta, "Have you never gone in the church?"

"Yes, quite a few times… mainly for the Christmas Carol services… but I can't remember the altar looking like the standing stone in the picture."

"It'll be laying on its side, of course," her Nan pointed out, "And they probably squared it off a bit. And it is covered by the altar cloth during services anyway."

"We would like to see it!" suggested Rietta with Carla nodding for emphasis.

"Well, now we've been talking about it," agreed Nanna Ivy, "So would I." She stood up adding, "The vicar is one of those that believes churches should always be left open – a gesture of trust in god and humanity – so he rarely locks the doors. Only had the silver candlesticks nicked a couple of times." She smiled, "So, as they say, no time like the present."

As they left the house, Rietta's Nan paused to lock and test the front door.

"Don't you trust in god and humanity, then?" asked Carla.

"Well, I always believe the best in people, but it is prudent to remove temptation, I think. Besides, even the Vicar has taken out insurance."

Chapter Fifteen

Going to Church

It was a short, ten-minute walk to the church. It was a short, ten-minute walk to nearly anywhere in the small village. The church was built from large, chunks of granite. Their size was random, but each had been hewn into a squared block that fitted neatly with its neighbour. At one end, a square tower rose above the slated roof and the silhouette of a bell could be seen through an arch on each side. The church was quite large, for such a small parish, but was made to seem smaller by a tall and broad yew tree that grew in one corner of the churchyard.

The morning rains had wet the ranks of slate headstones so that they now caught the bright sunlight like mirrors. The uneven diamonds of glass in the big arched window also sparkled with reflected sunshine that changed through a rainbow of colours as they approached.

The door was old, weathered wood with a heavy grain and the heads of big black iron nails stood out in rows across its surface. Rietta turned the black iron hoop that formed a handle and heard the latch lift with a muted squeal, on the other side. She pushed, but the door did not budge.

"I think he's locked it, today…"

"No, c'mon, all together!" and with that Nanna, Carla and Rietta all leant their shoulders against the wood and pushed. The door swung slowly open, grinding across the grey stone floor beyond. The interior of the church was a dramatic interplay of light and shadow. Beams of vibrant colour shone from the big stained-glass window and painted the grey stone walls and polished wooden pews with blues and yellows and glowing pools of fiery crimson.

The floor was of large stone slabs as were the walls. Many of these slabs were deeply engraved with texts and designs. A row of arched recesses ran along each side, containing small, bright windows, and above them hefty black wooden beams supported a vaulted ceiling of plain white plasterwork. Some of the beams had grotesque faces or strange animals carved at their bases and winged heads of angels at the apex where they met.

The trio moved eastward down the aisle towards the biggest window, only just able to discern the dark mass of the huge altar through the dazzling spectral beams of light that fanned out before them. The slabs they walked over were badly worn, but were obviously ancient tomb markers, with barely legible names and dates carved into their surfaces. One was embossed with something that may have been oak leaves and a cluster of three acorns, another with a rather clumsy skull-and-cross-bones design. Unlike the headstones outside, these were not slate, but blue-grey stone that seemed to have been sparsely dusted with glitter.

The altar was no longer covered by the heavy red cloth that was reserved for services, its only covering now was a disk of white linen in the middle, fringed with gold brocade and centred with a simple silver cross.

They saw that the exposed alter was roughly hewn from a single monolith, bigger than a bed. The top had been levelled and was almost smooth, polished from centuries of use. The sides appeared to be raw, natural stone, with some evidence of crude chisel-work, though a design had been carved across the entire front face.

The bright daylight streaming from the stained-glass window threw the carving into high-contrast relief. Groups of simple figures stood to each side of a roundel containing a Celtic-style cross, its arms made up of intertwining lines that resembled tangled vines. The figures were primitive, with small stiff bodies and huge heads carrying grim expressions. Some of the figures held croziers – the stylised shepherd's crook sometimes carried by high-ranking church officials.

Carla had approached the altar and tentatively reached out a hand to touch one of the figures. It was its oddness that had attracted her attention, "Look at this one…" she said, startling herself, and the others, with the loudness of her own voice in the quiet. The figure she indicated seemed to have a head made entirely of leaves.

Amongst the figures on the other side of the roundel, Rietta had found another odd one out. She spoke softly, almost a whisper, "And this one's wearing antlers…"

"Mmm," her Nanna nodded with interest, bending to have a closer look, "It's all carved in the medieval fashion. We know the first stone church was built before the fifteen-hundreds, but I think the art looks even older – it has a Celtic look to it… What do you think it is a picture of?"

"Looks like a May-Day parade," guessed Rietta.

"Yes," agreed Nanna, "Does look like some sort of festival, doesn't it?"

"That cross looks like it's on a big circular door," observed Carla, "and the people are going to go through it…" she looked sidelong to catch Rietta's meaningful glance.

They lingered in the church long enough for Rietta to roughly sketch the altar, in situ, and draw some more detailed versions of the figures from its frontage. She had detached several pages from her sketchbook and showed Carla how to take rubbings by holding the paper against an embossed pattern and using a crayon, side-on, to make gentle, even strokes across its surface. A print of the design beneath seemed to magically appear on the paper.

When they had later returned to Rietta's for tea, both girls soon became aware of an odd atmosphere as they quietly ate their homemade sourdough pizzas, piled high with sauce, singed peppers – both red and green, sweet onion rings, baby corncobs and pale chunks of melty cheese. They recounted some of the discoveries they had made at the church and Rietta's mother and father nodded with interest, but made minimal comments in response. They seemed to have something on their minds…

After dinner, and before being offered dessert, the girls found out what had been distracting Sally and Henry, throughout. With trepidation, they followed Henry upstairs and to Rietta's room, where he simply asked them to explain how the hefty boulder happened to be there.

"I was drawing it…" Rietta said, rather lamely.

In a disturbingly flat and calm tone, Henry said, "I asked how, not why. You could not have carried that up here on your own…"

"We could have used the wheelbarrow," suggested Carla.

"Rolled it on, like we did when we found Scrufty?" Rietta added in support of the idea.

"Levered it up the stairs," expanded Carla, "One step at a time."

Henry's expression seemed to soften a little as he listened, weighing up the feasibility of what he was hearing.

"Yes," added Rietta, warming to the explanation, "We were taught Mechanics in Physics class… all about levers and pulleys, mass and momentum… stresses and forces…" her voice trailed off.

Henry eyed them both in turn, he did not wear a convinced expression, and sighed, "Well, even that was really dangerous. It's very heavy and if you'd lost control of that on the stairs… well, it could have rolled down and crushed one of you… I'm surprise you didn't break the stairs!"

"It could've gone through the floor!" added Sally from the doorway, in the throaty voice she used to indicate resigned exasperation, "This is an old house, you know. Old boards…"

"Sorry," said Rietta, sincerely, "It should be easier going back down."

With teamwork, the four of them did manage to utilise the wheelbarrow again and clunk the bulky rock down the creaking stairs, the wheel thudding on the carpeted steps one by one. Rietta and Carla were wondering if the mokrok would be jolted awake and reveal itself, but it remained stoically stone throughout its unceremonious eviction from the Harvey household.

Henry trundled it along the garden path and tipped it out of the wheelbarrow onto the lawn near the gate. Rietta and Carla had followed and as he turned to them he said, a little breathlessly, "Sketch it by all means, but it stays outside…"

Both girls gave suitably serious nods. They noted that the mokrok had rolled and come to rest on what they thought was its head.

Whilst Henry was putting the wheelbarrow away in the lean-to, Sally had gone in to begin preparations for dessert. Rietta and Carla loitered for a while and then made a pretence of leaning on the garden gate watching the low sun send golden searchlight beams between mountain peaks to sweep across the valley.

Talking without raising their voices, they tried to tell the mokrok what they had discovered, about the altar in the church being the standing stone they were looking for: the waystone.

"Are you awake, mokrok?" Rietta wanted some sort of response, "Lee, did you hear us?"

A muffled whisper replied, "When the night ends… I go. Meet you at church… in the morrow. Then we go… yes?"

"Tomorrow, at the church," confirmed Carla.

Rietta simply said, "Tomorrow…"

Chapter Sixteen

Preparations

Carla had heard the front door to the maisonette clunk closed before dawn. Her aunty was on the early shift, but Carla roused herself and got up straight away, for this was the day. Maybe. The day that would finally bring her dreams to reality…

She ate buttered toast for breakfast whilst cutting more thick, uneven slices of wholemeal bread, just how she liked it. Then, still chewing toast and drinking orange juice, she set about making cheese and pickle sandwiches. They only half-filled the Tupperware box and so she wedged a bag of crisps and an apple around them to prevent them sliding around and breaking up.

Then, back in her room, she changed out of her night shirt, put on a pair of skinny jeans and pulled on her favourite practical top, a long tabard with a geometric floral print in warm colours. With her bob of hair that shone like burnished mahogany and her wide, dark eyes, she thought it made her look more oriental. It left her arms bare, but she pushed her purple summer-weight hoody into her bag along with her packed lunch, just in case it got chilly where they were going. Though, in her dreams, the weather in the land of the fairies had always been fair.

Across the town, Rietta was also making similar preparations. After an early breakfast of porridge, she too set about selecting suitable attire... It was lightweight enough for summer wear. Tough enough to play in and smart enough for company – that is why it was her favourite dress. Deep blue with cap sleeves and buttons all down the front covered in gold twine that were almost impossible to do and undo, but she only needed to manage the top one to slip it on and off over her head. It was more of a tube than a dress, but there was enough flower and foliage embroidered down the front panels to make it look like the kind of dress that may have been worn by a proper lady in an old painting.

"I'm meeting Carla and we're going to have a picnic in the churchyard..." she reminded Sally, who was fumbling around the kitchen, still sleepy in her cosy panda onesie. "...we've been researching it at the library..." she folded the foil over the salmon paste sandwiches she had prepared for herself, "And it's like the oldest building around. I think I am going to use it for my history homework – we have to do a project on some aspect of local history. Everyone else is going to do the slate quarries or the sugar trade, so it'll be a bit different," tucked in the folds at each end to form a silvery-shiny brick, "And Carla is helping me with it, because she doesn't have the homework, but she'll be starting in my year after the summer!"

"Remember to take your sketchbook."

"Of course!" she grabbed it and stuffed it into her rucksack alongside the sandwiches and a couple of fruit juice cartons. Then she gasped, charged upstairs and grabbed Smugly. He was her long-time lucky charm and stalwart friend – he had to come too. With the floppy dog safely in the bag, she zipped the zipper, fastened the buckles and hiked the rucksack onto one shoulder.

"Good morning, dad!" she chirped as he too came down the stairs, still slapping aftershave lotion onto his pink cheeks, "I'll see you later…"

"Take care, sweetheart!" he called just as the front door was closing.

There was a boulder sitting in the grass just inside the gate to the churchyard. It had not been there on their previous visit and they recognised the quartz fissure and pattern of mosses.

"Well he's here, like he promised…" said Rietta, crouching down and patting the top of the rock three times.

No response.

"I think we'll have to wake him up again," suggested Carla.

"OK…" mused Rietta, "How do we do that, then?"

"Do we need the wake-up-a-mokrok rhyme?"

"Well it was the fairy-calling that did it last time, so maybe it's part of the magic we need to open the waystone…"

They took their positions to either side of the mokrok-stone and held hands over it. For a moment they looked into each other's eyes and then nodded when they were both ready to recite the rhyme. They closed their eyes and in sing-song voices spoke the spell in unison, "On gossamer wings, As the mistle thrush sings, You live in our dreams, Now become real things…" They opened their eyes and watched the rock.

No response.

Carla shrugged and ran her fingers through her hair, looking perplexed.

Then, Rietta's eyes flashed with an idea, "I know!" She dropped to her knees and, cupped her hands to the boulder and spoke into them, "Lee! Wakey-wakey, Lee!"

Moments later, there came an odd, dry creaking sound, like crushing soft chalk onto slate. The cracks and striations across the boulder began to shift and widen and parts of the rock pulled free. Rietta stood back, allowing the mokrok room to unfold. First a stubby arm on each side, then fingers unfolded and flexed. Then the top of the boulder began to lift and the head rose beneath its cowl of thick moss. The pale pebble eyes opened under heavy granite brows and the creature took in its surrounding for a few moments before resting its stony gaze upon the nearby girls. The lower half of its craggy face cracked a crooked smile, "Well, hello there, young ladies!" it croaked, "I take it we are ready to make the journey?"

They said, "Hello, Lee," to the mokrok. They were both nervously excited, but unsure of what else to say, and both were only half believing they were about to travel to another world through the ancient altar of an old church. They began leading the way up the narrow path of worn stone slabs. The mokrok dutifully followed, its brow ridges alternately rising and falling as it looked from one girl to the other. When they were about halfway along the path, the church door suddenly opened with a grinding creak and out stepped a tall and slender old lady, squinting at them through the bright daylight. She left the big church door ajar behind her and approached the trio. Her walking stick was decorated with tiny metal shields and badges that glinted as is swung with every, measured stride. She was wearing a white cardigan over a blue knitted skirt and a blue floral headscarf covered her hair.

"What a strange and singular grave marker you have found there…" she lifted her stick, indicating the motionless mokrok, which had managed to step off the path and had frozen in the act of hunching around itself. With eyes, nose and mouth tightly shut and arms folded in, it looked like a primitive carving. A thin smile flitted across the woman's heavily rouged lips, "Strange, I've never noticed it before… must have walked past it hundreds of times…" she looked back to the girls and stepped closer, "Sometimes it takes another's eyes to make you see the familiar afresh, does it not?" The girls simply nodded politely. "Evidently, it has been around a long, long time," she gave a little chuckle, "Perhaps even longer than I have."

"Yes, er, it is…" began Carla, and Rietta finished the sentence, "…very unusual. Could be mediaeval…"

"Indeed?" the old lady arched a drawn-on eyebrow.

"We're doing a history project," Carla explained more confidently.

"For school," Rietta added, trying to, make it all sound convincing.

"Well, then you must go into the church and have a look at the remarkable altar. That is certainly very, very, old – built the church around it, or so I have been told…" she paused with a smile in her eyes, "Ah-hah!" she exclaimed, "I am a poet and I didn't know it!"

The two young girls glanced at each other and smiled back. The mokrok remained stone-still between them, eyes and nostrils shut tight. Rietta was wondering how long it could hold its breath in mokrok form, or if it had changed back to its real-rock form once more.

The lady observed Rietta intently, eyes narrowing as if she should really be using spectacles, "You're the Harvey girl, aren't you?"

"Yes. That's right," Rietta replied, casually brushing some strands of her fine fair hair from before her eyes, "and this is my friend – she's new here."

"Well, well…" the lady smiled so that her perfect dentures glinted, "You're a big girl now, aren't you!"

"My Nan says I get bigger every day…"

"I dare say that you probably do, Miss Harvey," she gave a little nod to Carla and said, "And I'm pleased to meet you, Miss New-Here." The lady let her smile linger a moment longer as if awaiting some response, then said, "It's nice to see youngsters taking an interest in the church… Well, well… lovely day for it!" She squinted around the church yard and then turned to move on, pausing to add, "Say 'hello' to your Nan for me, won't you?"

"Yes, I will!"

They watched her walk carefully along the slabbed path towards the gate and out of the churchyard. She turned left at the gate and they continued to watch as her head and shoulders seemed to slowly glide along the top of the neat hedging and disappear from view behind the great yew tree.

Carla lent in at Rietta's side and whispered, "Who was that?"

"Mrs Thomas. I think she does the flowers… Jake, her grand-son, he goes to my school."

The mokrok's gravelly voice cut in, "Me gets the feeling you had not checked the church was empty, before you awoke me."

"OK, I'll check it is now," volunteered Carla and skipped up to the hefty dark door, put her shoulder to it and pushed it open a little wider. Seconds later, she reappeared in the doorway and beckoned them in.

* * *

Inside, the air was fragrant with the scent of fresh flowers drifting from bouquets at the end of each pew and the larger arrangements in window recesses along both sides. The stone-on-stone footfalls of the mokrok echoed in the otherwise silent church as, flanked by Rietta and Carla, he waddled up the aisle toward the ancient altar.

"Conditions are very perfect, I suppose," said the mokrok, ascending the steps to the altar, his face tilted to the brightly glowing stained glass window, "Sun on high? Huh-humm," his neck creaked as he nodded, "that looks like correct position. Time is right. You know what they say, don't you?" He turned his head to give the girls a questioning glance over a broad, mossy shoulder.

"What do 'they' say?" asked Rietta.

"Every day is a gift – and that's why it is called the 'present'!" he gave his gravel-in-a-bag chuckle, "And there is no time like it!"

"So," Carla jigged with excitement, "What happens now?"

"We must open the waystone," the mokrok said very matter-of-factly, "Or else you will just be banging heads on a big stone!"

"And how," asked Rietta, "Do we do that?"

"Three things required," the stumpy stone creature turned to face them, framed in the round design at the centre of the altar-front, the strange processions of carved figures spreading to either side of him, "You need the keeper of the waystone – that be me. You need those willing to pass through the gate – that be you. You need the waystone key…"

"Key?" both girls said together, sounding perplexed.

"What key?" asked Rietta, an edge of disappointment creeping into her voice, "No one said anything about needing a key!"

"What kind of key?" asked Carla, "Where do we get it?"

The mokrok shrugged, his stony face seemed to hold a grin, "Me, I'm just the mokrok, Lee, humble gate-keeper, I do not have a key… but you do?" The girls gave him blank looks, his grey eyes flicked from one to the other as he continued, "A glyph? A rune? A sigil? A seal? Usually upon a parchment… or an amulet?"

The girls just shrugged, their faces were clouding over with anger-edged frustration, "We don't have any 'key'!" complained Rietta, her voice raised enough to echo back to her.

"What you woke me with…" suggested the mokrok.

The girls were quiet for a moment as they thought, "What? Our initials in twigs?" Rietta sounded incredulous.

"You showed me," stated the mokrok, jabbing a knobbly-knuckled finger up at her, "In your book of sketchings."

Realisation dawned across Rietta's face, first her eyes widened, glittering with colours reflected from the window, then her lips curled up into a smile. "Yes!" she exclaimed, "I have that with me!"

She easily shrugged the rucksack from her slender shoulders and swung it gently round onto the steps between her feet and where the mokrok stood. In moments, she had reached out her sketchbook and opened it to the page where she had drawn the design based on the way Carla's initials and her own fitted so neatly together. They formed what looked very much like a magical symbol. "You mean this?" She held it up in front of the mokrok's face, which lit up with pale light reflected from the paper.

He nodded, and said cheerfully, "Then this is it, now…"

"So what do we do?" asked Rietta, bubbling with enough enthusiasm to push any apprehensions aside.

The mokrok held up a hand and counted things off on his fingers, "Waystone… Gate-keeper… Those wishing to pass… that's you, yes?" The girls nodded eagerly and he continued, "Gate-key… Solstice sun on high…" He seemed to enjoy delaying the proceedings. "So," he said finally, "All is ready."

"So, tell us what we have to do," Carla prompted.

"Simply place the key upon the stone," the mokrok shuffled to one side and rested one of his broad hands flat on top of the altar, "and wish it in your mind, to pass through…"

Rietta glanced at Carla who nodded in agreement, then she placed her sketchbook onto the altar, pages open at the motif.

Moments passed.

Nothing happened.

"Other way up, perhaps," suggested the mokrok as if patiently instructing a toddler, "So stone may see key."

Rietta flipped the open sketchbook over so it now lay pages down against the stone top of the huge altar stone. Instantly, there was a sound like a deep exhalation. The petals of all the cut flowers were ruffled by an invisible force, as if an unfelt breeze had rushed through the church towards the altar. Moments later, the air began humming with a deep, almost subsonic tone, as if heavy machinery had started up somewhere deep in the crypts below. The throbbing hum rose up and through the floor and now seemed to come from the altar itself. The simple silver cross vibrated and turned slightly upon its circle of gold-fringed linen. The huge waystone-altar glowed softly, as if lit from within, and in seconds it became as bright as any of the windows.

"Well, now, there you go…" the mokrok's voice seemed distorted and almost lost in the deep rumbling vibrations that pervaded the church, "The Way is Open!"

"So we just…" with the fingers of one hand, Carla mimed walking across her other palm.

The mokrok nodded, "You want to take that?" He was looking at Rietta's rucksack, which she quickly re-shouldered. He gestured with his free hand, as if politely holding a door open for someone to pass, "Good luck, girls. Be seeing you, on the other side."

Carla reached out to Rietta and they took hold of each other's hands. The smiles had faded from their faces. They exchanged serious glances and then stepped up to the glowing monolith. There was just the slightest hesitation before they took a final step, fully expecting to kick their toes on hard stone. Instead, they saw their feet pass through the carved front surface of the altar, followed by their lower legs. Their four eyebrows shot up with surprise as their unseen feet found nothing to stand on. It was as if the whole altar had become an open trap door in the floor, and with short gasps of surprise, they both pitched forward and disappeared through it.

A message from the Red Sparrow

We hope you enjoyed this book enough to want more...

As a small independent publisher, The Red Sparrow Press is always very grateful for positive reviews and social media support. So, if you would like to read more of Rietta's and Carla's adventures across the Three Realms, please let us know. Better still, let your friends know!

If you, or your folks, could find a moment to write a little review on amazon, that would really help us out! Or simply spread the word - the Red Sparrow has a twitter account (of course) so please tweet us @RedSparrowPress and let us know your favourite bits, or share some of your drawings inspired by the fantastic fairytale you have just been reading...

We'd love to hear from you!

Parts two, three and four will follow shortly, but in the meantime, read on for a special preview of THIS part two, as things become even more magical… and more perilous…

PART TWO

Over hill, over dale,

Through bush, through brier,

Over park, over pale,

Through flood, through fire,

I do wander everywhere.

WILLIAM SHAKESPEARE

A Midsummer Night's Dream (1605)

Chapter Seventeen

Another World

There was a flash of golden light followed by the strange sensation of slowly falling into deep darkness. It was as if they had jumped into something like water but thicker and at body temperature so they could hardly feel it. For a moment the girls' grip on each other's hands slipped and they were alone. Panicking. Falling. Unable to see anyone or anything else. An infinite black void. Not even able to see their own limbs flailing in so solid a darkness. The emptiness carried no sound, so their screams were silent. Spinning and reaching out they found each other again, only inches apart, and each flung their arms around the other. Then the void lurched like an elevator suddenly slowing... An instant of weightlessness before they landed heavily, flat on their backs, the jolt knocking the breath out of them.

They had both screwed their eyes shut against the utter darkness and now a rich crimson light glowed through their eyelids. Their eyes opened wide and so did their mouths as they gulped in cool, deliciously fresh air.

They were on their backs, looking up at the leaf-laden branches of a great tree, an oak. Shafts of sunlight slanted through like searchlights. Birdsong and the lazy buzz of insects drifted from all around.

"You OK?" they both asked, and answered, "I think so."

"I think it worked…" said Rietta incredulously.

Carla sprang to her feet, saying, "Oh yes, it worked…"

Rietta took Carla's hand and pulled herself into a sitting position to take in their new surroundings. "…most definitely…" she affirmed, letting her rucksack slip from her back.

Around them, a carpet of tall bluebells broke through the dry leaves of the forest floor, scenting the air strongly and sweetly. They were in the midst of a lush woodland, shaded by the great oak which, by the girth of its mighty trunk they knew must be truly ancient, perhaps older than a thousand years – and it was not alone. They were surrounded by trees of equal stature, with moss covered trunks standing like pillars of some vast natural cathedral. The woodland floor was a contrasting patchwork of great ragged shady patches and pools of sunlight, glaring with the greens of shrubs and their neon-bright, multi-coloured blooms.

Rietta's sketchbook was laying in the leaf litter at her side, she picked it up and her smile of wonder faltered, "Where's the mokrok?"

Carla shrugged, still scanning their surroundings for any sign of him. Her gaze came to rest on a fallen bough, festooned with clusters of ivory white mushrooms, which lay nearby. A bird was perched upon it, regarding them with shiny black eyes. It looked like a bluetit, but it was closer to the size of a chicken. It hopped down and tossed dry leaves about as it moved closer, tilting its head one way then the other to peer at them with each beady eye in turn. With a flutter of wings, it perched onto Rietta's rucksack and chirped surprisingly loudly, then, more surprisingly still, it spoke, "Crumbs? Crackers? Cheese?" it chirruped, "You have seeds?"

The girls were dumbfounded for a moment, until Carla managed to say, "Hello – we have some sandwiches…"

"Are you our new guide?" asked Rietta, hopefully.

The bird flicked its wings and bobbed up and down a couple of times before singing a series of tuneful, chirpy tweets.

"Was that your name?" she asked.

The bird bobbed again in a way that seemed to be a 'yes'.

"Well, I'm Rietta," she said with a wide smile, "and this is –"

"– Carla," she crouched down and politely offered her hand in greeting, "Pleased to meet you, Chirpy!"

The bird hopped off the rucksack to inspect the hand more closely, obviously expecting to find food in it.

"Sand-witch-yes?" it cheeped.

"Can you take us to the Fair Ones?" asked Rietta, earnestly.

"Here I am," stated the bird, simply, as it hopped around them, "Home here. I eat seeds. Eat nuts. You have? Seeds?"

Rietta gestured to the abundance of flowers and gleaming forest fruits they could see around them, "Looks like plenty more seeds on the way right here."

"Seeds?" the bird said again, recognising the word and sounding very hopeful.

Carla grinned and glanced across to Rietta and whispered, "I don't think he's our guide."

She delved into her bag and produced her Tupperware lunchbox, took out a sandwich and tore it in half, handing part to Rietta. They intended to break off chunks and throw them to the expectant and persistent bird, instead he hopped onto Carla's knee and took a beakful of bread and cheese directly from her hand, then hopped across to Rietta's shoulder and took another chunk of what was on offer, chirping, "Cheese, cheese, cheese," as it did.

The girls laughed at its antics and when it had joyously devoured the sandwich, Rietta suppressed her giggles to ask, "So, any idea which way we should head off?"

"Go find nuts?" He cocked his head quizzically.

"We could do with finding the mokrok," added Carla, "Have you seen a mokrok?"

"I eat seeds!"

The girls could not help laughing, Rietta managed to say, "We need to find the Fair Ones, or find someone who can help us to find them…"

The bird did another leaf-scattering hop-around, clicking and chirping, "I tell Jack," and with that fluttered off, its wings flashing through the patchwork of light and shade, disappearing into the woodland deep.

Rietta grinned broadly and said, "It most definitely did work!"

"Absolutely," agreed Carla, "but what has happened to our mokrok?"

Rietta stood up and offered Carla a helping hand to hoist her from her crouching position, and said, "He must need to find his way, from wherever his stone is… looks like we came through somewhere unexpected."

"Mmm…" Carla looked around, nodding thoughtfully, "and I don't see any standing stones round here."

"Perhaps it's because the waystone in our world had been moved out of position."

"Which means he could be anywhere."

"And, far as we know, we are anywhere else!"

A butterfly, with dazzling wings the size of dinner plates, fluttered down into a nearby clearing. The incandescent reds, blues and yellows blazed in the sunshine as it alighted on a huge, curving arch of bramble, lazily opening and closing as it enjoyed a warm rest.

The girls both gasped in awe and Rietta said, "Have you seen the size of those blackberries, too!"

"Is everything here super-big? Or, do you think it's us who are small?"

"You think in this place, we're all tiny and fairy-sized ourselves?"

"Maybe it works that way," considered Carla, "– they seem small in our world, but in theirs, it's the other way around."

"Well, then, let's hope we only meet seed-eating birds!"

In silent agreement, they decided to get closer to the resting butterfly for a better look. Taking short, careful steps, they approached the more-than-healthy briar patch. The stems of the brambles were as thick as a big man's thumb, some as thick as a wrist, with dark, plumb-coloured thorns that gleamed in the shadows crowded with clusters of big shiny black fruit.

They stopped short of the bramble-clogged clearing, transfixed by the beauty of the spectacular butterfly. As they watched, wide-eyed, it took flight again. Their faces dimmed for an instant as its shadow passed over them. It flew so close above their heads that they could feel the draught from its wing beats ruffle their hair. They both made breathily impressed noises and watched it flit a slow spiral up and away towards the sunny sky above the leafy canopy.

Her blue eyes bright with wonder, Rietta turned back to the clearing and saw that a particularly large and shiny specimen of blackberry hung close by, very near the edge of the big briar patch. The middle of the patch was impenetrable, with stems arching well above head-height, but near to the edge they were less than knee-high. Although the thorns were bigger, they were fewer and further apart than those on the brambles that grew in the woods back home. She was sure that she could reach.

With care, she placed her feet into the spaces between the thick stems and in just a couple of steps, the beautiful berry was in arm's reach. A loud rustling from deep within the patch made her pause mid-reach, her smile of delight faded to a frown of apprehension. Was a jealous wood mouse coming to defend its bounty? Or did those shadows at the centre conceal a spider in proportion to the other creatures they had seen? A spider that was now closing in on her?

"Rietta!" Carla's voice had an unmistakable edge of panic and, when Rietta turned to quickly hop out from among the brambles, she found herself looking back at her friend through a curtain of twisting stems that had reared up, snake-like, from under the dry leaf-litter.

The whole briar patch was now in motion. Stems passing over stems, weaving a complex curving network of thorny green, rustling and creaking against each other as they rose up and surrounded her like a cage. Some of the wrist-thick stems curved over and back down, their huge thorns passing very close to her frightened face. At times like this, she would expect to scream, but instead a deceptively calm-sounding, "Oh, no…" came from her throat as she was forced to lean back to avoid the moving thorns from catching her flesh. She was soon in a contorted posture and knew she could not keep her balance for more than a few seconds. Younger, suppler stems had closed around her ankles and were spiralling up her legs. She felt their needle-sharp spikes prick her skin as they tightened.

Carla was pulling at the briars, trying to grasp between the thorns, but there were already several scratches around her wrists where she had misjudged the motion of the plant. Her face was stern with determination, but also reflected the fear her friend felt.

"Don't let it get you too!" called Rietta, trying to sound brave, but the brambles seemed to be focussing their attack only on her, with Carla's efforts having little or no affect. The cage grew ever tighter.

Then the woodland shook, and there was a dry roaring noise as, nearby, a whirlwind sprang up from the forest floor. Fallen leaves rose up in a tight column that reached the lower branches of the trees, where it then pulled in swirls of fresh green leaves. In a matter of seconds, it became clear that a figure had taken form in the centre of this sudden storm. It seemed to be made of the leaves themselves and soon settled into the shape of an impossibly tall man. The last few leaves were still circling when a voice rushed out from the figure. It was a voice that sounded like a gale in the treetops and all the birdsong of the dawn chorus rolled into a few syllables from no language the girls could recognise. The sound was at once both beautiful and terrifying.

To Be Continued…

The Red Sparrow Press

P O Box 1, Blaenau Ffestiniog, LL41 3ZB, United Kingdom

THIS © 2016 Jeremy Dean & Hazel Cariad

THIS © 2016 The Red Sparrow Press

All rights reserved

No part of this book may be used or reproduced in any manner without prior written permission from the publisher except in the case of brief quotations embodied in critical articles and reviews. This book is supplied subject to the condition that it shall not in whole or in part, by way of trade or otherwise be lent, resold, hired out, transmitted, stored in a retrieval system, or otherwise circulated without the publisher's prior written consent in any form or binding or cover other than that in which it is published and without a similar condition including this condition being imposed on the subsequent purchaser.

'The Red Sparrow Press', the 'Red Sparrow' logo and all components thereof are singularly and collectively trademarks of questing beast.

This is a work of fiction. All characters and scenarios are fictitious.

The publisher and other contributors do not and cannot warrant the performance or results you may obtain by using this text. There are no warranties, express or implied, as to noninfringement of third party rights, merchantability, or fitness for any particular purpose. In no event will the publisher or any other person or company be liable to you for any consequential, incidental or special damages, including any lost profits or lost savings, even if the publisher has been advised of the possibility of such damages, or for any claim by any third party.

ACKNOWLEDGEMENTS

Cover illustrations by Remy Dean

Formatting by TypoTyke

Set in Book Antiqua

This, *Part Two* of the epic fairytale fantasy by Remy Dean with Zel Cariad, available now…

Printed in Poland
by Amazon Fulfillment
Poland Sp. z o.o., Wrocław